"There is another course of action we might pursue. Though I fear, Majesties, it will be even less to your liking. . . ."

✤✤

At these words, a silence fell upon us. A terrible silence, like a blight.

I knew what the soothsayer meant. We all did. If the spells spoken over me in my cradle were fulfilled, the calamities which threatened to destroy us all would stop. All it would take was the prick of a finger. Followed by one bright drop of my life's blood.

I heard a rustle of garments as my father moved to stand beside me and my mother. "I want you to go back to your room and get a good night's sleep, Aurore. Don't let the ramblings of frightened fools keep you awake. In the morning, we will decide what must be done."

And though he turned away swiftly, he was not swift enough, for I saw the thing that was in his heart.

Grief.

For his own fate. But even more, for mine.

BEAUTY SLEEP

Cameron Dokey

SIMON PULSE
New York   London   Toronto   Sydney   Singapore

First Simon Pulse edition December 2002

Text copyright © 2002 by Cameron Dokey

SIMON PULSE
An imprint of Simon & Schuster
Children's Publishing Division
1230 Avenue of the Americas
New York, NY 10020

Designed by Debra Sfetsios
The text of this book was set in Adobe Jenson.

Printed in the United States of America

2 4 6 8 10 9 7 5 3

Library of Congress Control Number 2002110490

ISBN 0-7434-2221-X

BEAUTY SLEEP

❖ Table of Contents ❖

❖Preamble❖

I've heard it said (though I can't say whether or not it's true) that all good stories begin in the same way, with the exact same words.

Since I naturally want you to find my story a good one, one that keeps you reading as much for the comfort of familiar details as for the new ones that surprise you, I've decided to stick to tradition.

You know the words, don't you?

Of course you do.

Once upon a time . . .

There. Thank goodness that's over with.

Now that I've gotten the traditional opening off my chest, I'm free to tell my story any way I want to. Because isn't that at least part of the reason for telling your own life story? To tell the truth at last. Your truth, your way. Not the truth other people think you should tell in the way they think you should tell it. Which is really just another way of saying the way that makes them look best and feel the least uncomfortable.

1

Stories are tricky things, aren't they?

Because the thing about them is that the same events can be told any number of ways. It all depends on what you think is important, and, when the important stuff is happening, whether you're looking directly at it or looking away.

Here we come to my first true confession, which, coincidentally, may also be my story's first surprise. (By which I mostly mean that it surprises me.) Now that I've actually used those words (*once upon a time*) I have to confess that they don't seem so stupid and traditional after all. Actually I kind of like them. They have a certain ring. They conjure, like a spell. And I suppose the fact that I'm not the first to use them doesn't automatically make me unoriginal. Isn't it the words that follow *once upon a time* that make a story truly come alive?

All right. That settles it. If I'm going to tell my story (which I am), I want to tell it right. So I think this means I need to start over, this time really believing in *once upon a time*. Believing that it will draw you in, take you with me to a place you've never been before. (You only think you have—a thing that may well be my story's first surprise for you.)

I know.

Close your eyes. Now conjure up your favorite door within your mind. Perhaps it leads to a room you visit everyday. Or maybe it's for special occasions, the place you go to be safe and warm and comfortably alone. Perhaps the door is actually a garden gate, an entryway to a place filled with the mysteries of living things. Perhaps it's simply the front door to your own home. Are you going out, or going in? Never mind.

I'll tell you about the door I conjure. It is made of old, dark oak with iron handles and hinges. Not fancy, but sturdy and serviceable. A trustworthy sort of door. You know what lies beyond it, don't you?

That's right. My truth. My way. My story.

Can you feel its unseen forces gathering around you? The handle of the door slips from your hand and the door, my door, begins to open wide. Before you realize what you've done, you've accepted the invitation, put one foot across the threshold. That's all it takes. You're in for it now.

Begin at the beginning, the place where all good stories start.

You know the way. Of course you do.

❖One❖

Once upon a time

  ... and so long ago that the time I speak of can be remembered only in a story, a virtuous king and queen (my parents) ruled over a land that was fair and prosperous (though it wasn't all that large).

Their kingdom being at peace, and their people being well fed and content, you might think the king and queen would be so also. But alas, it seems they were not. (Content.) For they lacked the one thing which would make their happiness complete: a child.

For years, the king and queen had dreamed and waited. Long years, and so many of them that, one by one, their hopes for a child began to pack their bags and depart. And this stealing away of hope eventually took its toll. It compelled the king to do a thing he did not wish to do, a thing he never would have done, had he not lost hope for a child of his own. He named his younger brother's son as his heir apparent, the brother being deceased and therefore not available himself.

The boy's name was Oswald.

Not that anybody ever called him that. His propensity for skulking in corridors the better to learn other people's business (particularly their secrets), combined with his habit of playing nasty practical jokes based on what he'd learned, had earned him a nickname.

Everybody called him Prince Charming. Because he wasn't.

After many years of wishing for a child to no avail, a terrible day arrived. This was the day the king and queen awoke to discover that all their hopes were well and truly gone. But this turned out to have an unlooked-for benefit, for the absence of hope left a vacuum, a void. And now I'll tell you another thing I've heard said, and this I know is true: Nature hates a void. As soon as one occurs, something has to rush in to fill the empty space, for that is the way nature wants things to go.

And so it was that the void created by the desertion of their hopes turned out to be the best possible thing that could have happened to my parents. For in hope's absence, a miracle arrived.

On the very same day that she realized all her hopes had fled, the queen also realized she was with child. A thing that, when she informed her husband, caused both their hearts to fill with joy. So much so that all their hopes heard the ringing of it, halted in their flight, turned around, and raced right back home. Between their hopes, their miracle, and their joy and wonder at both, my parents' hearts were therefore filled to overflowing before I was even born.

Many great things were predicted for me. Naturally, I would grow up straight and true, for that is what's supposed to happen when you are born royal. I would be beautiful if a girl, handsome if a boy. Above all, I would do my duty. First, last, always. When I put in my appearance on the exact same day the royal soothsayer had appointed, this was taken to be a sign that I would fulfill all these predictions, plus many more.

Several years and many disappointments later, my mother would be overheard to remark that the day of my birth was the only occasion she could recall on which I had been dutiful according to her definition. When my father protested that she was being too hard on me, she settled for the unarguable statement that it was most certainly the only occasion for which I had ever been on time.

In spite of all that happened later, every account I have ever heard concerning my actual birth relates that Papa and Maman were so delighted that a child had arrived at last that they were willing to overlook the fact that I was a girl and not a boy, boys being the preferred rulers of kingdoms, as you must know. For reasons that my nurse once explained to me were largely reproductive, but that I don't think I'll go into here and now.

I was born on a bright but chilly day in late September. Nurse has told me that my very presence warmed the room, for, even then, my hair was bright as the dawn. It made such a perfect arc around my head that it resembled a halo, an aureole. A combination of circumstances that caused my mother to immediately proclaim that the only name which could do me credit was Aurore.

This though she and my father had discussed naming me after his mother, whose name had been Henriette-Hortense. But, as my father was not about to deny my mother anything in the moments immediately following my birth, that plan was abandoned and the deed was done. From that moment forward, I was called Aurore.

It was, and still is, the custom in the country of my birth to hold a christening when a babe has reached the age of one month old. How this period of time came to be decided upon isn't clearly remembered, but it's generally assumed that the reason is twofold. A month is long enough after the birth so that a baby no longer appears quite so wrinkly and red, thus sparing those who come to congratulate the new parents considerable worry in the way of coming up with compliments on the beauty of the child. A month is also thought a long enough period to determine whether or not the infant is a good match in temperament for the name bestowed upon it shortly after its arrival. Many are the girls who are born Charlotte but end up as Esmerelda. Or the boys who begin life as Wilfrid but end up as just plain Bill. Well, not many, perhaps. But some.

In my case, however, there was no possibility that I might, even yet, become Henriette-Hortense. My hair having apparently grown even more golden with each passing day, and my eyes even more blue and my skin more rose petal–like, according to the nurse, anyway, the matter was considered settled. I was to be Aurore. First, last, always

You know about my christening, of course. Everybody does.

Or the bare bones of it, anyway. What went right. But mostly, what went wrong. Given the size and scope of the event, what seems most incredible to me is that my parents never saw the disaster coming ahead of time. It's been suggested they were dazzled by the gold of my hair. (Though, now that I think about it, I seem to remember that this suggestion came from Oswald.)

What I do know—what everybody knows—is this: When the invitations were sent out, for the one and only time in her life, my mother failed to manage a social engagement to perfection, and her list was one person short. Not just anybody. *Somebody.* By which, of course, I mean Somebody-Who-Proved-To-Be-Important, even if that wasn't how she started out.

Who she was has been greatly distorted. Most versions of my story say she was an evil fairy and give her some fantastic name, usually beginning with the letters *m-a-l. Mal*, meaning bad, which over time has come to mean the personification of evil, just as Aurore has come to be the personification of all that is beautiful, innocent, and bright. I am the candle flame snuffed out too soon; she, the years of impenetrable dark.

This is for the simple-minded, I suppose. An attempt to show that she and I were opposites right from the start. All pure nonsense, of course. Not only didn't people think she was evil, they didn't think of her at all. And that, I believe, was the true heart of all the trouble that followed.

Her name wasn't "mal" anything, by the way. It was Jane. Just that, and nothing more. (And, for the record, there are no fairies in the land of my birth. They prefer the land just on the other side of the Forest, *la Forêt*, a place you'll hear much more about before my tale is done.)

After the big event, by which I mean my christening, people discussed Jane's life in great detail. Though I suppose I should say at great length, because there weren't really all that many details. Or none that anyone could accurately recall.

It was generally agreed that she was related to my mother, a distant cousin of some sort. And that she had been part of the entourage accompanying Maman when, as a young princess, she had come from across the sea to marry my father. There were even those who claimed to remember that Jane had been a member of the actual wedding party, that she had followed behind my mother, carrying her train. But when I asked Maman about this once, *she* claimed to have no memory of whether or not this was so.

When I remarked, very curious and a great deal put out, that it seemed incredible to me that Maman should be unable to remember whether or not a member of her own family had taken part in her wedding—been assigned, in fact, the important responsibility of keeping the bride's elaborate train straight and true during its long march down the aisle—my mother replied that she had been looking forward, not back, on her wedding day. In other words, her eyes had not been fixed on Cousin Jane. They had been fixed right where they should have been: upon my father.

Not long after, she sent me to bed without any supper for speaking too saucily, which was her way of saying I was asking too many questions, and furthermore that they were uncomfortable ones. This was neither the first, nor the last, time this happened. Nurse often remarked that I owed my fine figure not so much to all the time I spent outdoors, but to all the times I had spoken saucily to Maman.

Regardless of whether or not Cousin Jane actually took part in the wedding, on one thing everyone concurred. After the wedding, Jane simply dropped from sight and was forgotten. Or, more accurately, perhaps, she found a way to blend so perfectly with her surroundings that she became someone others completely overlooked. Everyone, in fact, except (perhaps) for Oswald.

Now we come to some important questions, ones to which we're never likely to have answers as only Jane can provide them, always assuming even she knows. The things I've always wondered are these:

Did Jane *choose* to become invisible, or did it happen on its own, because of who and where and what she was? It's pretty plain she must have been unhappy for a good long while. But was her invisibility a cause or a result? Was it her unhappiness's root or vine?

Here's my theory: It was both.

I don't know how the world works where you live, but the place where I grew up is steeped in magic. This actually explains why ours is a place fairies don't call home. They prefer a more everyday place, where their own magic can have greater impact. There's magic in the air we breathe, the water we drink. When we walk, magic rises upward from the ground and enters our bodies through the soles of our feet, even when we have our stoutest boots on.

In other words, it's everywhere. In the wind and the rain. The feather from a bird that you find in a field during a country ramble. The hard, uneven surfaces of city street cobblestones. If you've grown up here, you're used to it. It's just the way things are. Almost everyone who's a native can do some sort of magic, even if it's something simple like boiling water for tea in the morning while you're still in bed, instead of having to crawl out of your warm covers to stir up the coals.

If you haven't grown up here but come to live, one of two things can happen, of course: Either the magic leaves you alone, or it doesn't. And if it doesn't, it does the same thing to you as to the rest of us: It makes you more of what you are.

This is a thing about magic that is greatly misunderstood. Magic isn't all that interested in change, which explains why things like love spells almost always backfire. And why those of us who grow up with magic don't use it nearly as much as people who haven't might think. (The boiling of tea water aside.) Nothing about magic is simple or straightforward, to be used lightly. And it's definitely not a substitute for what you can do just as well with your hands and your mind.

The people who end up with the strongest magic are the ones who are quickest to recognize this. Who see that magic's true power lies not in attempting to bend it to your will but in leaving it alone. Because if you do that, you'll discover an amazing thing. The will of the magic becomes your will of its own accord. For magic is a part of nature. It, too, hates a void. And the voids magic most wants to fill are the spaces that exist inside a person. It longs to strengthen that which is only waiting to be made strong.

Have you ever heard it said that somebody has shown her or his true colors? That's exactly what I'm talking about. The thing that interests magic is your true colors. Who you really are. And it can make you more powerful only if you first accept this. Which means, of course, that you have to be willing to accept yourself completely. Your virtues and your flaws. Most people shy away from doing this, another reason why magic doesn't get used as much as you might suppose.

But not Jane. She must have looked at herself without flinching. Unlike my mother, who has no time for magic, thereby making sure it has no time for her, Jane soaked it up, like a stunted plant in freshly watered ground. And herein lies magic's greatest danger. Remember what I said about the way it strengthens that which is waiting to be made strong?

If your virtues make up your true colors, that is well and good, for you as well as for the rest of us. But what about those whose true colors are comprised mostly of their flaws? These are the ones most likely to use magic for evil, even if they're not evil to begin with. For the things within them that the magic strengthens are like hunting knives: double-edged, wicked-sharp, and strong. They stick deep, cut both ways, are honed by power and pain alike. Such things cannot be held inside forever. Sooner or later, they must be released or they will slice their own way out.

What better way to release pain than to take revenge on the people you believe have wronged you? An eye for an eye. A tooth for a tooth. My power casts down your power, if only for a moment. Your pain replaces mine.

If Jane had been invited to my christening, who can say how much longer she would have held her pain locked up inside? Who can say what might *not* have happened? But she wasn't invited, and so something did.

"Little Princess, lovely as the dawn. Well-named Aurore."

This is what she is supposed to have said when, the last in a long line of wish-bestowers, she stood at my cradleside. By then, a horrible hush had fallen over my christening, a clotting sense of dread. Nobody recognized her, you see. Or (perhaps) nobody but Oswald. But her malice, that was an easy thing to recognize. Nurse has told me that the very air turned hot and tingled, the way it does right before a thunderstorm. You just knew that something bad was about to happen, she said.

As it happened, she was right.

"Yet even the brightest of sunrises must come to an end. *Tant pis*. Too bad," Cousin Jane went on.

Then, before anyone could prevent her, she reached down and scooped me from my cradle, holding me above her head so that her face looked up and mine looked down. I reached for her, my small fingers working to take hold of something, anything, for I wasn't all that sure that I liked my present situation.

At this, Nurse says, Cousin Jane smiled. As if I, myself, had provided the final inspiration for the pain she was about to unleash upon us all.

"Your end will come with the prick of a finger," she said, as she slid one of her own into my fist and I held on tight. Though everyone but Nurse has told me this is impossible, I swear I can actually remember this moment, what her finger felt like. Smooth and cool, but not the smoothness of skin. I know that now, though I didn't at the time.

Several years later, when I was judged old enough

14

not to choke myself on it, I was given a chicken drumstick as a special treat at a picnic we were having on one of the many palace lawns. Any opportunity to get messy always delighted me, according to my mother, and all went well, until I'd gnawed my way down to the bone. At the first touch of it, I became hysterical, and it wasn't until several hours later that Nurse finally managed to calm me down enough to tell her what was wrong.

That's what Cousin Jane's finger had felt like. Not smooth skin, but the smooth caress of cool, hard bone.

"The prick of a finger," she said again, giving hers a little shake, as if everyone hadn't heard her the first time around. "One sharp wound. One bright drop of blood. That's all it will take to cut your life down. Sixteen years, I give you, *ma petite Aurore*, lovely as the dawn. The same number I was given before I had no choice but to follow your mother to this gilded prison, so far from my home."

There was a moment of stupefied silence.

Then, "*Jane?*" my mother gasped out. A question, an uncertainty, even now.

At which point Cousin Jane tossed me high into the air and swept my mother a bow. "Well met, Cousin," she said. "You will remember me from now on, will you not?"

With that, she vanished in a puff of smoke, through which I plummeted straight down into my nurse's desperate arms. Behind her, she left just the faintest tang of sulphur, and the ghost of a laugh that never quite died. It lingered in the air, like an elusive smell. Vanishing for days, for weeks, on end, only to creep around a corner and assault you when you least expected.

Haunting us all for more than a hundred years to come.

❖ Two ❖

Maman swooned, of course.

She always does what a lady is supposed to do, though, to be fair, on this occasion even I must admit her behavior had good cause. For many moments, all was pandemonium. But at last, I was restored to my cradle, Maman to her senses, and the guests to relative calm.

Interestingly enough, it is Nurse's recollection that the person largely responsible for the return to order was Oswald. This in spite of the fact that he was only ten years old. Whether he performed this good deed out of the goodness of his heart, or from some other motive, I cannot say.

Though the goodness of his heart theory seemed doubtful to me for many years. Before you can act out of the goodness of your heart, it helps to actually have one.

But it was after order was restored that the next dreadful thing happened, because it was then that Maman said: "Do something, someone."

A thing which probably doesn't seem so bad, unless you understand that what she really wanted wasn't for somebody to *do* something, but to *undo* it. Specifically, of course, to undo what Cousin Jane had

17

done. And even this probably makes perfect sense to you—why not do everything you can to undo a great evil? Why not just erase it if you have the power?

The thing is, you can't just go around undoing other people's magic. In the first place, it's considered terribly impolite, not to mention impractical. If you do it to someone else, what's to stop them from doing it to you? Before long, you'd have absolute chaos.

There is a more important consideration, of course.

If you start undoing magic, *any kind of magic*, you run the risk of undoing everything else. That's how tightly magic is bound up in the way things are where I come from.

And so my mother's request, so reasonable on the face of it, actually contained within it the seeds of the direst consequence: the unraveling of the way our world is woven. Because, as even the world's clumsiest weaver can tell you, you can't pull on one thread without affecting all the others.

Everyone who heard her plea knew this. Indeed I think she knew it herself. I also think she simply didn't care at that point. She'd never been comfortable with magic. Always, it had seemed unnatural to her. As unnatural as having your wish for a child snatched away almost as soon as it had been granted, for example. If that was the way the world worked, why not unravel it and start again?

"Do something, someone."

At least she didn't ask my father. To have begged

18

a king to make a choice between saving his daughter or saving his kingdom would have been a dreadful thing. One that had the power to tear his heart apart without any magic at all. And I think my mother knew this, and wished to spare him. For she truly loved my father. Their long years of waiting for a child had drawn them closer together, not pushed them farther apart.

So it wasn't to my father she turned in her desire to erase what Cousin Jane had done. It was to her closest friend and number one lady-in-waiting: my godmother, Chantal.

No, she was not a fairy godmother. There aren't any fairies where I grew up; how many times must I tell you? But it is true that Chantal was generally acknowledged to have the most powerful magic in all the land, stronger even than my father's. And all of it good. Her true colors were as bright and clean as the colors of a rainbow. If anyone had the power to undo what Cousin Jane had done, it would be Chantal.

I often wondered, as I grew up, what her answer must have cost her. And the thing about understanding yourself, knowing your true colors, is that you have to be true to them. For if you don't, they change, and so do you. And so there was really only one thing my godmother could reply.

"I cannot do what you ask, Mathilde. What is done cannot be undone. You will know that if you think reasonably for a moment, just as you will know how sorry I am to answer you so."

But my mother was beyond reason. "For pity's sake, Chantal! This is my *child*. Your godchild," she cried. "Does that mean anything to you?"

"Of course it does," my godmother answered in a voice that Nurse told me once sounded like and old piece of wood. "But this child is not worth unraveling the world for. No one is."

My mother struck her then. In anger, in pain, and in despair. If Chantal would not save me, no one could. And how much worse must it have been for my mother to hear my doom pronounced not by an enemy, a stranger, but by someone she knew well. Someone she trusted and loved.

"Leave me," she said, in a voice that sounded as if she had something hard and sharp stuck in her throat. "Leave this kingdom and don't ever come back."

Nurse has always maintained Maman took another breath, intending to say more. To proclaim a dire end should Chantal disobey her, should she dare to show her face anywhere within our borders. If she would not commute my fate, then hers would be to suffer a death sentence of her own.

But at that moment, Papa intervened. Not with words, for that was not his way. He simply placed a hand upon my mother's arm. As he did so, my mother swallowed the sharp thing inside her throat and her words choked off.

My godmother showed her true colors to the last. She gave my mother one perfect bow. Then she slowly walked down from the dais where she had been standing behind my mother's throne, toward where my cradle rested at the bottom of the steps. As she did, there occurred something odd. She began to weep. Not that that is strange in and of itself, but as her tears struck the marble steps, they made a clatter. All looked, and were astonished at what they saw.

For Chantal was weeping pearls so lustrous and fine their match has never yet been brought up from the depths of the ocean. At a signal from my father, attendants gathered them up. To this day, I have a necklace of them as tall as I am. But every time I put it on, the urge to weep becomes so overwhelming that I have never worn it.

When she reached my cradle, my godmother stopped and turned around, and bowed again.

"Your Majesties," she said. "All others here have given their gifts to the Princess Aurore. But I have not yet bestowed mine."

Though she had made a statement, my father understood that she was asking a question, and so he nodded his head, tightening his hold upon my mother's arm.

"If what is done cannot be undone, then let it at least be done again," said my godmother. "This child shall prick her finger at sixteen, but this need not bring death. Instead she will sleep for a hundred years, and be awakened by a kiss at the end of that time. If it's true love that awakens her, so much the better, but this is a thing I cannot promise. For true love comes when it will, not when it is called."

She ran a hand over my cap of golden hair, then leaned down low, as if her next words were for my ears alone. They weren't quite, of course, for Nurse heard them, which is how I know.

"May you keep what you hold in your heart safe and strong, *petite Aurore*."

Then Chantal straightened and looked right at my mother. "That's the best that I can do, Mathilde," she said. "Whether or not it is enough, only time and Aurore herself can show."

I've often wondered what my life would have been like if Maman had answered, if she had called Chantal back to her side. But she didn't. The sharp thing she had swallowed slid down her throat to her belly. There, it mingled with her pride. And so she let Chantal turn and walk away. None of us ever saw her again. Perhaps she found her place in another story, one with a happier ending. I hope so.

And this was Cousin Jane's greatest accomplishment, I sometimes think. More than the pain the threat of my death caused. By her desperate actions, she drove others to desperation, and so we came to be deprived of our brightest light, our purest colors. Our truest friend and best ally.

And, with Chantal's banishment, it may be said that I truly embarked upon the first ten years of my strange and unusual childhood.

❖ Three ❖

*D*o you have any idea how challenging it is to live your life deprived of sharp objects? To live each day as if the presence of a butter knife constitutes a threat?

Of course you don't.

Unfortunately, I do, so let me tell you this. A good time is *not* had by all. In fact, by hardly anyone. Sometimes I think the only person who really enjoyed those first years of my childhood was Oswald. And why should he, you might well ask. I know I did. *He* wasn't the one being reminded every day that *he'd* had two spells cast over him when he was only one month old.

The truth of the matter, as he often found occasion to mention, was that, in spite of my birth, Oswald's situation really hadn't changed very much. He was still my father's heir. For, as the years passed, Papa did nothing to change the decree of succession. In fact, contrary as this might seem, my birth might even have improved things for my cousin. I was only going to be around till I was sixteen, after all. At that point, something nasty was going to happen in spite of all my parents were doing to prevent it. Somehow or other, I was going to manage to stab myself.

(Oswald was particularly fond of this word. *Stab*. It had such a healthy, gruesome sound.)

The resulting wound didn't have to be very big. One bright drop of blood was all that was required to activate the spell(s). After which, I'd probably just fall right down on the spot. Saved from death, that much was true. But, in its place, condemned to the nap from hell. A hundred years is a long time to slumber. More than enough to give Oswald *and* his heirs time of their own. Time to consolidate their hold upon the kingdom that should, by rights, be mine when I awoke.

And then of course there was a possibility that could not be dismissed, according to my cousin anyway, and that was that I might not wake up at all. Who in their right mind was going to want to kiss someone who'd been sleeping for a hundred years? Would I still be young? Or would I age as I slept and so grow old? Chantal's counterspell hadn't been very precise upon that point, even I had to admit.

Not a very promising future for me, all in all.

Which brings me to a second set of things I've always wondered: Did Oswald and Jane know each other? How much of what happened at my christening did my cousin know about ahead of time, even though he was just a boy?

There is no proof they knew each other at all, of course. Or none except the way the certainty of it, the rightness, seemed to ring in my heart like a great bronze bell.

Here is what I think happened: They met by

accident, Jane and Oswald, in some musty little-used corridor. Or perhaps it was in Oswald's favorite hiding place, the one that enabled him to overhear the most secrets. He simply turned around, and there she was. For it has always seemed to me that their magic was complementary. A perfect fit, like the way Oswald's hand looks in one of his immaculately tailored kid gloves.

His great talent in those early days was for uncovering secrets. Hers, for being a secret in and of herself. What could be more natural than that they should discover one another? And that they would be drawn together having done so? It made no difference that he was young while she was grown. Kindred spirits are what they are. Their talent lies in recognizing their own true colors in another, and this recognition forms an unbreakable bond.

Perhaps Cousin Jane did what she did for love of Oswald. Who can tell? Certainly not I. Or perhaps she simply saw a way to hurt my parents and at the same time benefit the only person in all those years to have seen her truly. Perhaps it is even the case that her motivations aren't really all that important in the long run. She did what she did, then left the rest of us to deal with it. But there is no denying that the one who came out best was Oswald.

I probably don't have to tell you that I did my best to stay away from him. Most of the time, it wasn't really all that hard. In the first place, he was much older than I was. Eight when I was born. A gap that pretty much guaranteed we'd never have much in common, even if we were fond of each other.

Which we were not.

But about the time I turned ten and Oswald turned eighteen, a funny thing happened. The only way I can describe it is that Oswald grew up. My best guess is that he simply awoke one morning and realized that things might be better for him if he was known as Prince Charming for a reason other than the current one.

Not because he was so obviously *not* charming, but because he so obviously *was*.

I think it was right around this time that my nurse began to tell me bedtime stories featuring the adventures of various leopards who tried to change their spots. Unsuccessfully, I hardly need add.

Oswald had better luck. So much better that, before too long, everyone at court forgot that his nickname had originally been a cruel joke. Now the nobles called him Prince Charming because that's what they thought he actually was. Maman remained unconvinced. What Papa thought, he kept to himself. Chances are good I would have followed my mother's lead, had it not been for one thing:

It was Charming Oswald (as I preferred to call him) who finally convinced my mother to turn me loose in the great outdoors.

For years Maman had argued (with success) that the best way to hold the spells that threatened me at bay was to keep me indoors, as far away from unexpected things as possible. It was true that I wouldn't be able to engage in any of the more traditional forms of princesslike activities, including the thing at which she excelled: painstakingly boring embroidery. But there were other ladylike tasks I might pursue, such as painting bowls of fruit or braiding rugs to set before the fire.

No matter how many times I ate the fruit instead of painting it, usually getting juice all down my front, and no matter how many times my rugs contained gigantic and mischievous bumps that threatened to send anyone foolish enough to tread upon them hurtling headlong into the fire, Maman insisted that indoors was safer than out. For me, at any rate. There were simply too many surprises out of doors. And after all, as she was fond of saying, usually as a way to end one of our inevitable arguments, even a simple stick, properly wielded, is capable of drawing one bright drop of blood.

In vain did I vehemently protest and my father gently suggest that she was being just a tad overprotective. The spells spoken over me in my cradle weren't supposed to be fulfilled until I was sixteen years old. Couldn't I at least go out from time to time till then? Well-supervised, of course.

Her answer was always the same: No. No. A thousand times, no. And that was the way things stood, until Oswald managed his amazing transformation and became genuinely charming. And no sooner had he completed one transformation, than he performed another: He changed my mother's mind.

"Well," he said one day, a particularly fine one, as I recall. So fine it had provoked an unusually impassioned plea on my part to be let out, and an equally impassioned denial from Maman.

All this happened shortly after lunch. We were in my mother's solar, a bright room at the top of the tallest tower, the room in which we always sat when the weather was fine. The fruit that had not been consumed at luncheon was now arranged into an improbably artistic pile and prominently displayed in a dish on a sideboard. My paints and easel stood nearby. Maman glanced significantly at them both from time to time, while her fingers worked her current piece of embroidery.

I wasn't about to do what she wanted, of course. Instead, I sat on the windowseat beside my father and tried my best not to pout. Not that I held back from this as a rule, but I did not want to pout in front of Oswald. My father reached over and tousled my hair in an attempt to cheer me up.

"Really, Philippe," Maman protested at once. "You'll make her all mussy, and she does that often enough all by herself. You were saying?" she asked, switching her attention back to Oswald. Not that she really wanted to know what he would say, but giving him her attention was an excellent way to show she was put out with me and Papa.

"I was saying that I'm sure you know best, Aunt

Mathilde," Oswald said with an engaging smile. He really was astonishingly handsome, particularly when he smiled, a thing I may have neglected to mention before. His hair was everyday enough: dark brown. But his eyes were gray and flecked with gold. Like the ocean on a stormy day when the sun breaks through and flashes across the surface of the water for just a moment. When you looked at Oswald, you didn't want to look away. There was a thing about him that captured you and wouldn't let go.

At the moment, he was standing in front of the fireplace on what was, perhaps, the most unfortunate of all my rugs. Fortunately for him, there was no fire, as the day was so warm and fine.

"I refer, of course, to the matter of Aurore being allowed to go outside," he went on. "I might pursue a different course, if she were *my* child." Here a look of horror crossed his face, as if he realized he might have gone too far, and his words broke off.

"What different course?" my mother demanded at once.

A thing that might seem strange, on the face of it, considering she disliked Charming Oswald. But she disliked the thought that he might have considered something she hadn't even more. (A thing I'm absolutely certain Oswald knew quite well. My cousin was many different things, but stupid wasn't one of them.)

"It's just that it occurs to me," he said. He paused to flick an imaginary piece of lint from his sleeve and

Maman leaned forward as if spellbound. "If Aurore's activities were more . . . varied, she might actually be safer in the long run. Naturally, as her mother, you would not notice such a thing yourself, but the truth is—"

Here he paused again, this time to poke at the biggest lump in the rug with the toe of one perfectly-polished boot. "The truth is that Aurore can be rather clumsy at times." He raised those strange eyes to mine, the gold in them shimmering with mischief. "No offense, cousin."

I bared my teeth, wishing I could sink them into his leg. I might have been only eight, but I could tell that he was up to something. Usually this resulted in me being in trouble.

"None taken, cousin."

"Of course I know she is clumsy," my mother snapped, at which my father made a sound. "Surely that is all the more reason to keep her indoors."

"Well, yes," Oswald said slowly, this time paying great attention to the little finger of his right hand on which he wore the signet ring that had once belonged to his father. "If you say so. That is one way of looking at it, I suppose. But surely you'd hate for her to grow up ignorant as well. Anyone may be either clumsy or stupid by birth, but it's really too bad for a person to be both things at once. Unless they simply can't help it, of course."

My mother's eyes narrowed and I held my breath. Of all the signs that my mother was becoming angry, this was the most dangerous one. The one most likely to result in an explosion. Beside me on the windowseat, I could tell that Papa was holding his breath, too.

"Are you trying to say that my daughter is a dullard by birth or that I am raising her to be so?" Maman demanded softly.

"Oh, my dear Aunt Mathilde!" Oswald exclaimed, his expression horrified. He moved to her swiftly and got down before her on one knee. "Now it is I who have been dull and clumsy, for I have failed to make you see my point. I only meant that the more of the world Aurore knows, the less chance it will have to surprise her. For isn't that what we all fear the most? That her fate will take her unawares, and so overcome her?"

"*C'est exact.* That is so," spoke up my father.

"Well," my mother sniffed, with a sharp glance in his direction. "If you're going to take his side . . ."

"But surely it is not a question of sides," Oswald protested, at his most sincere and charming. "It is only a question of what is best for Aurore."

A silence fell as we all looked at my mother. I could see her turning Oswald's words over and over in her mind, the way a fast-moving stream tumbles a stone. Seeking out the rough places, scouring them smooth.

"You think that Aurore will be safer if she is allowed to go outdoors."

"I do," Oswald answered promptly. "Children are curious, Aunt Mathilde. They mean no disrespect to their elders in this. It is simply the way they are. Since this is so, why not let Aurore indulge her curiosity? Let her go outside if that is what she desires. If you don't, she'll only find ways to get into trouble where she is."

And it was this argument, so undeniably true, that finally won my mother over and changed her mind.

"Very well," she said at last. "Aurore may go out as long as she stays within the palace walls. But I really must insist . . ."

I never did hear what it was she wanted to insist I do. Or not do, more likely. Because by then I was off and running, out the door and down the long curving staircase that lead from the solar to the great hall. Across the hall and through a side door I knew led to the kitchens, though I had never been allowed to spend more than a few stolen moments there (too many sharp objects such as skewers and knives).

And then, finally, there it was: the great oak door that lead from the kitchen itself into the kitchen garden. As it was a sunny day and the kitchen was warm, the door was standing wide open. Through it, I could see the sunshine running over the garden like honey. For as long as I could remember, I had wanted to walk through this door. To pull radishes and carrots as I had seen the gardeners do from my bedroom window. To eat them with the dirt still clinging to them, not even pausing to wash them off.

❧ Three ❧

A pretty mundane place to want to begin my exploration of the great wide world, you may be thinking.

I can only say, with all due respect, that you would be wrong. There can be no better place to begin your exploration of the world than by stepping out your own back door.

The kitchen staff was well familiar with my longing to go out into the garden. They also knew it was forbidden, a thing that had always made them shake their heads and cluck their tongues. As I edged toward the doorway I heard Cook's voice say,

"You'd best stop right there, now, Princess Aurore. You know how your lady mother feels about you going outside."

"It's all right," an unexpected voice said. "Let her go." I jumped, for the voice was Oswald's. "*Madame la Reine* has changed her mind," he explained. "From now on, the princess Aurore may go into the garden."

At this, a spontaneous cheer swept through the kitchen, and I shot through the open door as if fired from a slingshot. I was so eager to explore everything at once, I ended up standing stock-still instead, simply inhaling the heavily scented air of the garden.

A thousand smells seemed to rush toward me at once, as eager to welcome me as I was to be among them. That one was rosemary, with its medicinal tang as sharp and pointed as its dark and shiny leaves. This, the musty pungence of oregano and thyme. Beneath them was a thick, rich smell that I imagined must be the earth itself. A scent that seemed to me to be the same as its colors, green and brown.

And over everything there lay a scent so sweet it made my head spin. Later I learned it was orange blossom. Just being able to stand in the sun and breathe it all in made me want to run around in circles and be still as a stone at the same time.

Though in the years that followed I went farther and farther afield, farther than I could dream was possible at that moment, in those first seconds of freedom, I had everything I'd ever craved. The kitchen garden was world and free enough.

When I finally did begin to move about, so engrossed did I become that it took me some time to realize that Oswald had followed and was watching from the arch of the open kitchen door. And there was in his face a thing for which I have no name even now, after all the years that have come and gone.

"Cousin, come and look at this!" I cried. And so he moved to kneel beside me in the garden, not caring that his perfect clothes got dirty in the process, a thing that, until that moment, I hadn't even noticed about mine.

I had found a plant whose leaves were pointed on both ends and broad in the middle. Bumpy top and bottom, colored green and purple all at once. I rubbed them, sniffing my fingers and Oswald followed suit.

"That is sage, Aurore."

"Sage," I breathed. A word I knew meant wise. "Do all the names of plants describe the hearts of men, then?" I asked.

And Oswald answered, "No, not very often. I think you've found the only one. Beginner's luck."

I pointed to a plant with leaves as green as spring itself, long and pointed as the tips of spears. "What is that?"

"That is tarragon."

Twice more I pointed, and both times, he knew the answers. "You know them," I said, and even I could hear my voice was filled with awe. "You know them all."

"No," Oswald said. "Not all, just some. If you want to know them all, we must get the head gardener for that."

I gave him a sidelong glance. "Or perhaps the gardener's lovely daughter."

Her name was Jessica. I'd seen her from my window and knew she was every bit as beautiful as her father's garden. Her hair was the rich dark color of the fertile soil. Her eyes were as green as the first leaves of springtime. I'd heard Nurse and my mother's lady's maid clucking their tongues over her and Oswald. He had his eye on her, they said. I wasn't sure what that meant, but it sounded suspicious.

Oswald reached out and tweaked the end of my braid which had, of course, begun to come undone.

"Very well," neatly calling my bluff. "Shall we call her?"

"Not today," I said swiftly. "Tomorrow." For tomorrow would be different. Still wonderful, yes. But not filled with this same wonder. You don't have to be a grown up to understand the way things change. To understand that a thing can be truly new only once, and precious because it came to you when you did not look for it.

"Today, tell me what you know. Please, Charming Oswald."

This time, he gave my hair a tug. "I hate it when you call me that."

"I know."

At that, the thing in his face for which I'd had no name became a thing I recognized, and that thing was a smile. "Just for today," I begged. "I won't ask again."

"Of course you will," he contradicted. "You're always asking for impossible things, Aurore. It's one of the very few things I like about you."

I sat back, intrigued. "Why?"

He was silent for so long I thought he would not answer, but finally he replied. "I guess because I want impossible things too, only I have never dared to ask for mine aloud."

"It doesn't do much good," I said, surprised to discover that I was drawn to console him. "I never get any of the things I ask for."

"You did today," said Oswald.

"Because of you," I answered. "Thank you, Charming Cousin."

At this I could tell that, for perhaps the first time in our lives together, I had surprised him. Pleasantly, I mean.

"You are welcome, *ma petite Aurore*. Very well, just for today then. I will tell you what I know. But don't expect me to be so nice to you everyday."

"Don't worry," I said. "I won't."

At this, Oswald laughed and stood, not even bothering to brush off his dirty knees. He extended one hand down. I reached up to take it. He wrapped his fingers around mine in a grip that was at once gentle and strong, and together we set off to explore the rest of the garden.

Though things between us would never be simple, there was a change from that moment on. He no longer tormented me quite so much, nor made quite so many mentions of my inevitable untimely end. And I no longer pointed out to him that, though he was my father's heir, he was still his second choice.

And there were many who remarked upon the fact that, when I discovered some new thing that I wanted explained or simply wished to share, I took my treasure first not to Papa or Maman, or even to my nurse, but to my cousin. And they remarked also that, whatever he might be doing, Oswald excused himself from it at once and remained with me until I had all the answers I wanted.

Whatever would come between us, sooner or later, nothing would ever be able to erase the thing that had been that day engraved upon my heart: It was Oswald who had won for me my freedom, the thing that I desired most.

And in doing this, he also brought about the third and last of his amazing transformations, for such things always come in threes, as you must know.

First, he changed himself. Second, he changed my mother's mind. And, finally, with my first step out of doors, he changed the inside of me, for he rewove the very fabric of my heart.

It still beat with a trip and a hammer, for that is the way a heart must go. But, whereas before it had woven only dark things when it dwelled upon my cousin, now within the fabric of my heart there ran, for him and him alone, one single strand of pure, untarnishable gold.

❖Four❖

The years that followed were the happiest of my life. Though I suppose I should say, the happiest until now. But the *now* that has but so lately come to pass was *then* so far away as to be almost invisible. The thinnest wisp of white cloud in a sky the same color blue as Maman's favorite china cups. I couldn't yet even imagine that *now* would ever be.

So I'll say it again:

The years that followed were the happiest of my life.

Oh, I still did plenty of things I didn't particularly want to, such as painting trees and wildflowers, for instance. Though even I had to admit this was an improvement over the never-ending parade of fruit still lifes. And there was one area in which as far as I was concerned Maman took Oswald's words a bit too much to heart. She now insisted that I learn to embroider, reasoning that the more familiar I was with my needle the less likely I would be to jab myself and so draw one bright drop of blood.

But, on the whole, things were so much better there is really no comparison.

Except for the nightmare, of course.

I suppose I should have expected there would be

a price to pay for my newly acquired freedom. But I didn't. You don't really stop to consider these things when you're only ten years old. I didn't yet perceive the way everything that happens is connected— didn't realize that opening a door that led to outside exploration would inevitably open a door to the unexplored places inside myself.

And, just as exploring the outside world brought new words to my vocabulary (*hyacinth, chamomile, mugwort*), so did exploring my inner world give me new terms to ponder. *Fear, confusion,* and *ambiguity* above all else. For, though I had certainly heard these words before, I didn't truly understand them until the nightmare began.

The dream was always the same, and I had it once a month. The day of the week varied, but the date stayed constant. The twenty-eighth. The same date on which I had been christened. This might not seem so bad to you. Just twelve nights out of a possible three hundred and sixty-five. But believe me, those twelve were more than enough. And the fact that the dream was always the same didn't make enduring it any easier. It actually made it worse, more inescapable, somehow.

From the time I was eight until I turned sixteen, the thing I dreamed every month, year in and year out, was this: I dreamed that I was someone else.

It unfolded gradually, like swimming through deep water, the way dreams so often do. In images that, from the moment they first occurred, always reminded me of a kaleidoscope. Clear one moment, distorted the next, until they finally settled into clarity again, having rearranged themselves into something else entirely.

I begin the dream by walking through the palace. A thing I've done every day for as long as I can recall. But a new, keen-edged sense of wonder and anticipation fills me. A sense of discovery seems to beckon me on. This is how I first come to realize that I am not myself in the dream. For I have never felt these things about the place where I grew up. For me, it has never been new, but always, simply, home.

No sooner do I realize I am not myself than the kaleidoscope of my dream performs its first revolution. The wonder of discovery begins to distort. It becomes a need, an insatiable hunger so strong I must obey it. And what it wants me to do is to run. As I do, I begin to weep. For it comes to me suddenly that I am searching for a thing I have lost. A thing that, though I cannot name it, I know in my heart matters more than anything else. But even as I wear myself out in the search for it, I know that it is lost forever. I will never be able to find it. It is irretrievably gone.

And as the kaleidoscope begins to turn again, I have one agonizing thought: that somewhere, in all the rooms through which I've traveled, I have lost myself as well.

Now there comes the part of the dream I hate the most. The part where I wish desperately to be awake, so that I could put a stop to everything simply by closing my eyes. But, as they are closed already, I am trapped. Try as I might, I cannot open my eyes and awaken, and so put an end to things that way. The dream is not yet ready to let me go.

For now the kaleidoscope revolves unceasingly, the images forming only for as long as it takes them to dissolve. I feel as if I am tumbling head over heels through the sky. It is dark one moment, filled with colors the next, until I lose all sense of space and time. But one thing always stays with me: the sense of pain, of loss. And as I suddenly see the ground rushing up to meet me I am filled with one desire: to make the whole thing stop, no matter what the cost.

I have heard Nurse say that, if you dream that you are falling, it is very important that you wake up before you hit the ground. Either that, or you must dream you land upon your feet, whole and unharmed. Since this is a nightmare, I do neither of these things. Instead the kaleidoscope turns again and, when it stops, I am lying flat on my face in the dark.

As I lift my head, light and color begin to return. I am in a room full of courtiers, dressed in their finest garments. They pass so near that I fear they will tread upon me, but somehow, they do not. I recognize many and I call out to them. Not one replies. But it isn't until I reach out to catch the silken hem of a passing dress that I realize why.

They cannot see me. I can no longer see myself.

I know that I exist. I can feel my churning stomach when I press a hand against it. Feel the hot stickiness of my own blood run down my face when I slam my head, hard, against the wall. But I can see none of these things. They are invisible, just as I am. Somewhere in the midst of my whirling tumble, I have been whirled right out of existence. Or, at the very least, right out of sight, of heart, of mind.

At this, so excruciating a pain fills me that an extraordinary thing happens: I wink back into being, as if this pain alone is the thing that gives me form. In that moment, I know I must carry it with me always, nurturing it like a child. Feeding it and tending it. I cannot afford to let it die.

For someday, I will find the way to make those who overlook me see me truly. Find the way to make them see the things I long for in my heart. And when I do . . .

I probably don't have to tell you that this is the moment when I always woke up, tears upon my cheeks, torn between relief and disappointment. Happy that the dream was over, it is true. But frightened by an outcome I could never see, and by a puzzle I have never been able to solve.

Who was I?

I can practically hear you say it. Surely the answer is obvious. I was Jane, of course.

This is what my nurse thought, for she said this is the way of strong magic sometimes. Nurse said that the strongest magic doesn't simply act upon us, it *becomes* us. Running with our blood, holding us upright from the inside out, just like our bones.

Two of the most powerful spells ever cast in the whole history of my father's kingdom were made over me. Now, according to Nurse, they lived inside me, constantly at war. One seeking my destruction, the other, my salvation. My nightmare was the inevitable result.

It made sense, I suppose.

Naturally, I tried not going to sleep on what I knew would be a dream night. It never worked. No matter what I did, sleep always came for me sooner or later, bringing the nightmare when it did. I suppose when the things that give you bad dreams live inside you, there's no point in trying to stop them. They're going to come out whenever they decide it is their time. Better just to close your eyes and hold on tight, the faster to get the things you fear to go back to sleep themselves.

I think the worst part is that when you know you dream another person's dream, you can never truly feel at peace. Never truly trust yourself. If you carry around somebody else's nightmare, who knows what else your insides might hide or when it might come out?

Now, where was I?

Oh, yes, the happiest years of my life.

They were, really. Nightmare aside. I got to go outside every day, usually for as long as I wanted. I started by exploring the closest places first. The kitchen garden, and then the other, more formal,

palace gardens. Naturally, my favorite one of these
was the one devoted entirely to roses, though it always
gave Maman fits when I went there. All those thorns.

But, finally, after several months, the day came
when I had explored every single inch of the palace
grounds to my satisfaction and was ready to take
the next step: the world outside the palace walls. I
wanted this so much it made my bones ache. So
much it kept me awake on the nights the dream
didn't come. Not in the same way. Not in fear, but
in anticipation. As if the wide world had a voice and
I alone could hear its call.

I was pretty sure I knew what Maman's reaction
to my going outside the palace walls was going to be.
As it turned out, it was Papa's reaction that provided
the surprise.

I've already told you three important things about
Papa and Maman. How they waited for many long
years to have a child. How they loved one another in
spite of this trial. How Maman preferred to define
her world with words, and Papa his with silence.
When Papa did choose to say what he thought, however, his words carried a weight Maman's did not.
This was not simply because he was king. It was
because everyone around him knew that, if he spoke
a thing aloud, it was because he had thought it over
thoroughly and made up his mind.

So when the day came when I could stand the
anticipation no longer and announced at dinner that
I wished to broaden my horizons, to go beyond the

palace walls, a look of horror crossed Maman's face and she pulled in a breath to give the answer I expected, which would have been: *"Mais non!"*

But before she could, Papa uttered this sentence. "Why do you wish to do such a thing, Aurore?"

At this, I became so astonished every thought flew from my mind. I had been prepared for a battle with Maman, not a discussion with my father.

"I don't know," I stammered out. "I just do, Papa."

Oswald's face assumed the expression it carries when I have done something particularly stupid, a thing that made me want to kick him under the table.

"But you must have a reason," my father urged gently. "I would simply like to hear it. There's no right or wrong answer. Take your time. Not everyone expresses an interest in spending time outside the palace, so I'm curious to know why you wish to. That is all."

Take that, Oswald, I thought.

I don't know how things are in the land of your birth, but in mine there is a division, *the great schism* Papa calls it, between those who live at court and those who don't. Those at court are mostly nobles, except for the servants, while those they refer to as the *common people* live outside the palace walls. In towns and villages. In the countryside. The nobles think as little about them as they can afford to, but in this they overlook an important fact of life: It is the ones outside the palace who perform the tasks which keep our country prosperous.

The nobles find no fault with the current arrangement. It's the way things have always been or at least for as long as they care to remember. Why should things not continue the way they are? The common people have come by their name for a perfectly good reason. Doing common labor is what they are good for, the only thing they know. Besides, it's so difficult to tell one from another. With their dirty faces and hands, they all look so very much alike. Better to pay as little attention to them as possible and let them get on with their duties. Better to stay within the palace walls.

Papa disagrees. He's the first king in nobody knows how long to do so. He goes out among the people, which is what he calls them. Either that or *my subjects*. Regardless of which it is, he never calls them common. He knows them by name, at least the ones in the village nearest to the palace. He takes time to listen to their sorrows and their joys. In short, he treats them like what they are: necessary and important, even if they aren't high-born. And the inevitable result of this is that, among them, he is greatly loved.

When Oswald was younger, my father often offered to take him with him when he left the palace. Always an opportunity, never a command. One which Oswald always declined. When it became clear that he would always do so, that his allegiance was to the nobles, my father stopped asking. And that is the way that matters stood during that dinner when Oswald was eighteen and I was ten years old.

"Aurore?" my father prompted softly.

"It's hard to explain," I said. "I think because it's so simple, Papa. I just know I want to go outside. It seems the right and proper thing to do."

"Yes," my father said patiently. "But why?"

"Because it does!" I exclaimed, feeling my face begin to color. This was becoming more dreadful by the moment. How did you explain a thing it had not occurred to you to question? A thing you just knew, clear through to your soul?

"The palace is wonderful and I love it," I said. "But it isn't everything. I know that there is more. The outside world calls to me, Papa. I *have* to go. I think it's because . . ."

I paused and took a deep breath. I'd said this much. Better just to get the rest of it over with quickly so Oswald could laugh and Papa could say no.

"Going outside is what I was born for. I can't explain it any better than that. I'm sorry, Papa."

During my ragged speech, my father had grown very still. Indeed, it seemed to me that for the space of time it took me to explain, he did not breathe at all, but sat with his head bent and his eyes closed. When I had finished, he exhaled one long, slow breath, sat up straight, and opened his eyes.

"I believe that explanation will do just fine, Aurore. Very well, since going outside is what you wish, you may accompany me when I ride out tomorrow."

With that, he signaled for the majordomo to serve the carrot soup that was the first course of our meal, Maman have been plainly rendered incapable of doing so.

I could hardly believe my ears. "You mean it?" I cried.

"Are you questioning me?" asked Papa. A thing that was unheard of. For a moment I feared I had offended him, for his tone was serious. Then I caught the twinkle at the back of his eyes.

"Absolutely not," I said. "I don't know what came over me."

"*Bien*," he replied. "That is much better. Now, eat your soup, Aurore. Carrots are good for you, and you will need all your strength in the world outside the walls."

For several moments, we all ate dutifully. No sound in the dining room other than the scrape of spoons against the bottoms and sides of bowls. But, little by little, I felt the air grow thick and heavy, as if, above our heads, it was filling up with storm clouds.

"There is one thing I would have you promise," Papa said, as the soup bowls were removed and a roast chicken was placed in front of him to carve. "Remember that to go into la Forêt is forbidden. You must promise me never to go there, Aurore."

"Of course I promise," I said promptly. A thing that was easy, for, in truth, I'd forgotten all about la Forêt until that moment. I'd have remembered it sooner or later, of course. Who wouldn't remember an enchanted forest? A thing Papa had obviously realized, for he knew me very well.

"I cannot help but wonder, Philippe," Maman said quietly, as if my father's mention of the Forest had given her the opening for which she'd been hoping, "whether taking Aurore outside the palace is such a good idea after all. The world is a very big place. There are many . . . unknowns."

"*Mais oui, bien sûr,*" my father answered, as he calmly picked up the knife and began to carve. "Of course there are unknowns. And the sooner Aurore begins to meet them, the sooner they will cease to be unknown. That is the point. Besides . . ."

He paused and set the knife down. I all but felt my ears prick up, the way the palace dogs' do when they hear an unfamiliar sound. *Something important is coming,* I thought. *Something Papa has been thinking over for a very long time.*

"For many years now we have let the spells spoken over Aurore in her cradle tell us who she is. Now the time has come for her to tell us who she is, as well. For we must never forget that, even if the worst happens and she sleeps for a hundred years, Aurore is a princess. She is royal, with a claim to the throne."

"But you have an heir," I said without thinking. "You have Oswald."

"That is so," my father replied, turning his eyes upon my cousin. "And I have been content to have him be so. But tonight you have done a thing Oswald has never done. You have shown a desire to know *all* those you might rule one day, not just those who are noble-born. More than that, you have told me this is a thing you *must* do. That it was for this that you were born. In this you have spoken like my true heir, for this is how I have felt, also."

By now the air in the room felt so thick, I was surprised I could still see through it. Across the table from me, Oswald clutched his fork so tightly his knuckles were white as mother-of-pearl buttons.

"You don't want me," he said, his voice tight. "You never have. You want Aurore."

"It is not a matter of what I want," my father answered. "It is a matter of what is best for the kingdom, best for all. Therefore . . ." He took a breath, and I knew in that moment we had come to the heart of what he wished to say. A thing that, since my christening day, he had been holding in his mind.

"Tomorrow, before Aurore and I set out, I will have you and your heirs proclaimed Aurore's stewards, Oswald. She will be my heir from tomorrow forth. It is Aurore who must succeed me, even if it takes a hundred years. Tonight, she has shown this must be so."

I heard Maman's swift intake of breath even as I felt my jaw drop open. It was a sign of her complete surprise that I managed to get it closed again before she could remind me that a lady never shows she has been taken unawares.

"For heaven's sake!" Oswald exclaimed. "All this simply because she wants to go outside the palace walls? She'll probably take two steps and fall into a mud puddle. Think what you are doing, Uncle!"

"What makes you think I have not?" my father replied. "If I had let my heart rule my head in this, I would have proclaimed Aurore as my heir the very day that she was born. But I did not. I waited—to see who you both would become. You have been content to see only what is before you. Aurore is not. That is all I need to know."

Papa's words were making my head spin, and not just because this was about the longest speech I'd ever heard him utter all at once. He was saying he thought I was worthy to be his successor. Even more, that he *wanted* me to succeed him, a possibility that had never occurred to me before.

And in that moment, I realized there was a thing inside me I had never thought to notice, probably because it had been there all along. And it was, greater even than my desire to see the world, the desire to be worthy of my father's faith and trust.

"All those years," Oswald whispered, and now the devastation was plain in his voice. "All those times you asked me to go with you when you left the palace, but I said no. You never urged me to change my mind. Not once."

"But surely you can see that I could not," my father said. "You had to wish to go for yourself, as Aurore does. Because it was what you wanted, not I."

"You tricked me!" Oswald protested. "You played a game with me, but never told me its rules. You played me false, Uncle."

"No, Oswald," said my father. "And I am sorry that

you think so. When you are calmer, I think you will realize I speak the truth. But I suppose it is too much to expect you to think so at this moment."

A thousand painful things seemed to chase themselves across my cousin's face, each one hard upon the heels of the one before it. Then, as if he had seized a curtain and yanked it across a scene he had never intended to reveal, his face went blank, though his eyes continued to smolder. I was glad he did not turn them upon me, much as I wanted him to know that I was sorry for what was happening. I had not known what Papa intended any more than Oswald had. But I greatly feared that he would blame me for it.

"Madame," he said to my mother. He pushed back from the table, tossing his linen napkin onto his plate. "The dinner you provide is excellent, as always. But I fear I may have suddenly become unwell, for I find I have no appetite for it. You will excuse me, I hope?"

My mother cleared her throat before she spoke. "But of course," she replied.

Oswald rose from the table, his back as hard and straight as iron. He bowed in turn to each of my parents, then gave me the lowest, most elaborate bow of all. He departed without another word, the heels of his boots striking so hard that sparks flew up from the flagstones.

"Well, that's that," my father said, when he had gone. "I suppose there was no way to avoid hurting him, but even so . . ." He broke off, shaking his head, then picked up the knife and began to carve the chicken once more.

"I hope you know what you're doing, Philippe," my mother said.

"*Bien sûr*," my father answered simply. "I am doing what must be done. It will be all right, Mathilde. You must trust me."

"I do. You know I do. But I hope to God you're right in this, Philippe," Maman replied. Her eyes stared at the door through which Oswald had departed. "He has the nobles' love. He has made it his life's work."

"He is like his father in that," Papa replied. "It may be enough for the son of a younger son. But not for one who will govern. The one who will do that must see beyond the palace walls."

"He would make a dangerous enemy," my mother cautioned.

"Then we must take care that he does not become one," answered Papa. "He is angry now, but his anger will pass. He is too smart to hold on to it for long. Now, if it's all the same to everyone else, I'd like to finish the rest of my dinner in peace and quiet."

"As you wish, Philippe," Maman said. And she held out her plate for some chicken.

But I said. "*Merci*, Papa."

At this, he smiled. "You are welcome, Aurore. But, I think it is I who should thank you."

"For what?" I asked in surprise.

But it was Maman who answered, and in a way which brought tears to my eyes.

"For growing up the way we hoped you might," she said.

After which none of us felt the need to say anything more.

❖Five❖

And so the next six years of my life began, with a proclamation read aloud the next morning from high atop the palace walls. In it, all my father's people learned that I would be his successor, no matter how long it took, rather than my cousin, no matter how great his charms, though naturally the proclamation itself was more diplomatic on these points.

The reactions to the announcement was predictable. Dead silence from the nobles inside the palace; wild cheering from the people outside the walls. For apparently the fact that my father loved me dearly and had cherished high hopes for my future was well known outside the palace. As well known there as it was little known inside. (Not because he had said this to anyone directly, I think, but because, to the people, this was the natural order of things. What should be so.)

When it was further announced that the king and his daughter would shortly be riding forth, the cheering from outside grew so loud as to be almost deafening, while the nobles simply faded back inside the palace like so many bugs crawling back into their holes.

If I had been wiser in the ways of the world, I

might have been more concerned about this. But I wasn't. I was only ten years old. Besides, I already knew the nobles did not love me. They had already given all the love they had to Oswald.

He stood just behind my father as the proclamation was being read, the counterbalance to the fact that I stood just in front of him. What my cousin was thinking, I could not tell. The curtain was still drawn across his face and now even across his eyes. If he was angry or hurt, dissatisfied in any way, he did not show it.

I hardly need tell you this day marked another change between us. I no longer went to him with things that interested me, questions to be answered, puzzles I needed help deciphering. For what else could they do but remind him of what he had lost? All the things he had not chosen? I caught him studying me from time to time, as, indeed, I sometimes studied him though I tried not to show it. Save for the times when functions of state required us to be together, we stayed apart. It was simpler all around if we avoided one another.

But I was not thinking of such things. Not on that first bright morning. For it was after the proclamation was read that my father gave the signal for the palace gates to be thrown open. Then, seated before him on his great gray horse, he and I rode through them together and out into the world beyond the palace walls.

I can still remember the quiet. The way more

people than I had ever seen before abruptly fell silent at the sight of me. Voices beyond my ability to measure suddenly hushing all at once. And twice as many eyes as that, fixed on the place where I sat before my father. I remember gripping the horse's mane so tightly the coarse hairs cut into my hands.

And then Papa said: "My friends, I give to you my daughter and heir, the Princess Aurore."

At that, a great shout went up. The women fluttered their aprons; men tossed their caps into the air; children jumped up and down. And I did a thing that surprised everyone, myself most of all. I tossed my leg over the horse's head, slid to the ground, and dashed straight into the crowd.

Years later, in a particularly cross and cynical moment, Oswald asked me how I had known to do this. For he claimed it was the best, most perfect thing I could have done. To run to them, my people, my subjects. To fly to them with outstretched arms. *I want to know you*, my action said. *There is no difference between us. We are the same, you and I.*

My only answer was that I hadn't truly known anything, not in a way that lets you plan things ahead of time. I simply did what my heart demanded. And, in this way, I answered the demands of my people's hearts as well.

The years that followed are one bright blur, in which I spent as little time inside the palace as possible. Instead, I learned to do anything in the world outside I could. No task was too menial, too dirty, too hard.

I learned to plow and plant the fields, not letting the fact that I sunburned my face and blistered my hands stop me. I held on until I developed calluses and my skin settled down to the color of toasted almonds. I learned to cut peat for fires and the proper way to thatch a roof. I fell off. Twice. The second time I broke my arm.

While recuperating, I spent time with the herbalist, learning which plants could bring down a fever, which could purge a stomach, which were best for the dying of cloth. I even learned which plants could be used to bring about a death, though I swore to keep this information to myself.

When my arm had mended, I learned to shear a sheep, to card and spin its wool. Lest I become too domestic, I also learned shoot an arrow from my very own bow and to throw a knife. Accurately in both instances. Though I never revealed these particular talents to Maman. Just as I never revealed the fact that, if I was doing particularly dirty or heavy work, I tied my hair back, stuffed it underneath a cap, and wore a tunic, boots and breeches, just like a boy.

In short, I pretty much stopped behaving like a regular princess altogether and had the time of my life. But there were two things I never forgot: la Forêt and Oswald.

My thoughts on my cousin, I kept to myself. For, though not precisely secret, they were certainly confused, a thing which kept me from asking him about la Forêt as I might once have done. After thinking it over for quite some time, I finally decided that the person who could give me the answers I wanted was none other than Papa. For had he not been the one to remind me the Forest was off-limits in the first place?

I waited until he was alone. Maman had still not quite forgiven me for the broken arm, and, if she learned I was interested in la Forêt, I half feared she'd shut me in my room and bolt the door. Papa often spent time in his study at the end of the day. It was there I sought him out one night when I was supposed to be in bed, being careful to first knock on the door. No one entered my father's study without his permission, not even Maman. It was his only private place.

"Come," my father's voice called.

I turned the heavy doorknob and pushed open the door. My father was sitting in a far corner of the room in a great chair made of dark brown leather. He had a book in his lap and spectacles perched upon his nose. He pulled these off and tucked them in a pocket as I came in.

"Why, Aurore. I thought that you had gone to bed."

"I can't sleep, Papa," I blurted out. "There is something I would like to know and not knowing is keeping me awake."

"This sounds serious," my father said, but I could see the way his eyes smiled. He took his feet from a low footstool covered in the same leather as the chair and gestured for me to sit down. "Have you come to tell me what it is?"

I nodded, and he gestured for me to continue. "Why is it forbidden to enter la Forêt, Papa?"

"Oh, Aurore." He closed his eyes for a fraction of a second, as if marshalling his strength, then opened them again. "I don't suppose it would do any good to mention how sincerely I have hoped you would never ask that question?"

"But you've made me your heir, Papa. I will be responsible for la Forêt myself one day. Don't you think its history is a thing that I should know?"

"You want to watch saying things like that," my father remarked. "It will make people think you're too clever for your own good. Not that you aren't right, of course. Very well. But don't tell your mother. She'll have my head."

"It shall be our secret," I vowed.

"La Forêt has been as it is for as long as I can remember," my father said. "Some would say for time out of mind. In my grandfather's time, there was a woman in the village so ancient none could remember her right name and so she was called *la Vieille*, the Old Woman. It was la Vieille who told my father what I am about to tell you.

"La Forêt is cursed, Aurore."

I felt something cold skitter down the back of my legs. "Cursed?" I said. "By whom?"

"According to la Vieille, by two great sorcerers,"

said Papa. "Where they came from originally, I cannot say. But they ended up here, in our land that is steeped in magic, for no other reason than to use it for their own purposes. To try to turn our magic to their will in a great contest."

"But why? What for?"

At this, my father shrugged his shoulders. "To prove who was strongest, perhaps. No one really knows."

"That's an awfully stupid reason," I said. "And if they were sorcerers they ought to have known better than to go messing around with magic that way."

My father's lips twitched, but he nodded gravely. "That is surely so. Is it said that the one who triumphed realized his folly in the end and, with the last of his strength, he cast a spell. One that contained the destruction, the unraveling, that had been wrought inside the boundaries of la Forêt. He could not heal it, but at least he could stop it from spreading any more."

"But what's wrong with the Forest?" I asked.

My father cocked his head. "I'm not sure *wrong* is quite the way to describe it," he said. "*Different* might be a better choice. The magic of la Forêt isn't like magic anywhere else. And remember it is contained. Folded in upon itself with nowhere to go. Even time moves differently there. For the magic of la Forêt doesn't need human minds to work its will. Instead it has a mind and will of its own.

"I've seen it snow beneath the trees on a warm

spring day. Placed a marker opposite a sapling one week, then returned the next to find nothing but a gnarled and rotting stump. La Forêt makes its own rules, Aurore. But what they are, it alone knows."

"Does no one ever go in?" I asked, for it seemed to me that, though he had warned me away from it, Papa himself had come very close.

"From time to time," answered my father. "According to la Vieille, if you enter the Forest with goodness in your heart, it will pretty much leave you alone. If you're lucky, it will even let you come back out again. But those entering it bent on mischief or destruction are never seen again. I hope you can see now why it is forbidden to go there."

"Of course I do," I said. "Thank you for telling me, Papa."

"Do you think you can sleep now?" my father asked.

I slid off the footstool. "Yes, Papa. I think so. And don't worry. I'll remember my promise." With that, I gave him a kiss good night.

"See that you do, Aurore."

And so my curiosity about la Forêt was satisfied, for the time being. And the tale my father had told me was enough to make even me leave the Forest alone. But I would be lying if I said that I forgot about it. Indeed, it sometimes seemed to me that the more I tried not to think about la Forêt, the more it took shape within my mind. It called to me, just as the world outside the palace had. Someday, it whispered, when the time was right, my moment to enter it would come.

And that is the way that matters stood when my childhood ended on the day that my sixteenth birthday arrived.

❖ Six ❖

Naturally, my parents insisted on throwing me a party. Equally naturally, I wished that they would not. The fact that I was turning sixteen might not be much cause for celebration, particularly when one considered what was supposed to be the year's inevitable outcome. But my parents were adamant, even Papa. It was important to honor this birthday, he said. Not only for itself, but to show that we were not afraid of whatever was to come.

Finally we compromised. They threw me two parties. One in the village, one in the palace. The first I enjoyed. The second, I did not. For it was at that party that it finally came home to me how completely unlike anyone else at court I truly was.

Not surprisingly, this revelation had to do with Oswald.

He was twenty-four now, well past time to be married. For obvious reasons, his choice of wife was considered of some importance and now, perhaps, time was running out. It was probably Maman who decided that, as long as we were throwing a party anyway, it might as well be used to parade as many eligible young ladies in front of Oswald as possible. But this decision produced an outcome Maman did not expect. Actually, two outcomes.

It showed Oswald to advantage, making clear how at ease he was among the nobles. What a catch he would be for any of their daughters. And it showed me to be his opposite. Out of place and frankly miserable. An odd duck in a sea of well-dressed swans.

I had attended court functions over the years, of course. I wasn't entirely ignorant of how to behave, though I was better at cutting peat than dancing a pavane. But the banquets or balls I had attended prior to this one hadn't been about me. For me. I'd been able to put in a brief appearance, perform what duty required, then escape to my room to plan my next day's adventure outside the palace walls. But this was an approach I could hardly take tonight, as the whole evening was in my honor.

It wasn't that anyone was rude. They wouldn't have dared, for one thing. If anything, they were incredibly polite. But it was this very politeness that finally first began to grate upon my nerves, and then to cause despair to rise up within my throat and threaten to choke me. For, no matter how smooth and correct the words issuing from the courtiers' mouths were, they couldn't quite hide the scorn or laughter in their eyes. And so, on the night of my sixteenth birthday, I saw myself as they saw me for the very first time.

My fingernails were clean, but my fingertips were stained a faint blue. I had been helping the village

weavers dye wool for winter cloaks. There were calluses upon my palms.

My hair didn't gleam like polished wood or stay
perfectly in place as the courtiers' daughters' did,
though it was true that it was still an almost impossible shade of gold. But all those years of being
stuffed inside a cap had given it a horror of being
confined and, over time, it had developed a will of its
own. No matter how many pins Maman and Nurse
jabbed in to hold it in place, my hair insisted on going
wherever it wanted. Usually, at unexpected and inop-
portune times.

On the dance floor, I forgot the steps and trod
upon my partners' feet, though, naturally, they were
too polite to comment. My new shoes, which
Maman had proclaimed were the height of fashion,
were just a shade too tight and pinched my toes. The
whole evening was like suffering through the clumsiest moments of my childhood all over again—this
time with the whole court looking on.

Finally, after a number of dances that seemed
interminable, it was deemed time to take a break for
refreshments and I sought a respite behind the column in the ballroom's farthest corner. What I really
wanted was to make a mad dash for my room, but I
knew there wasn't any point. Even if I would allow
myself to give in to such behavior, Nurse never
would. She would simply complete the evening's
humiliations by sending me right back down.

So I settled for tucking myself away, leaning my

hot face against the cool stone of the column and praying for time to speed up so that the party might be done. And that was when I heard a woman's voice I did not recognize say:

"But where is the guest of honor, the princess Aurore?"

I straightened up. It would never do to let anyone catch me moping. But, in spite of the defects the evening was making so clear, it was apparently easier to overlook me than I had thought. For a moment later I heard a voice say: "I do not see her." And this voice I knew, for it belonged to Oswald.

"How odd," the first voice said. "Surely she must wish to be the center of attention. I know I would, if the party were in my honor." Here, she gave a laugh like the tinkling of silver chimes in the wind. "But my father says there is no point in such a comparison, for I am not the least bit like her."

"In that, he is correct," answered Oswald. "You are nothing like Aurore."

Again his companion laughed, though this time I thought the sound was not so pleasing. "Tell me," she urged. "Has the princess grown as . . . unusual as they say? I myself have not seen her since we were both young girls, for I have been among my mother's people and have but lately returned to court."

"She is like no other," Oswald replied. Which only goes to show how good at court word play he truly was, for it wasn't really an answer at all.

"You must be such a comfort to the king and

queen," the young woman said, at which point I began to wish I could edge around the column without being noticed, the better to discover who she was.

There was a tiny silence. In it, I suddenly felt a lock of hair tumble around my shoulders.

"What makes you say that?" asked Oswald.

"Well, I mean, since their daughter is so . . . unusual," said the young woman I was beginning to think of as *l'Inconnue*, the Unknown. I'd never really minded the word *unusual* before. I'd rather liked it, in fact. But from her mouth, it sounded like an insult. What word might she have chosen if she were speaking to someone else? I wondered. One she had no wish to impress, and furthermore, one who was not my cousin.

"Surely the king and queen rejoice in knowing one as suitable as you will one day sit upon the throne," *l'Inconnue* went on.

There was a second silence, during which I felt another lock of hair come down.

"I regret to inform you that you are mistaken," Oswald said, and there was something in his voice I could not quite decipher. "I will be steward, not king. It is not my destiny to sit upon a throne."

"You think not?" *l'Inconnue* asked softly. "You seem to me to be no fool, my lord. Therefore, I think you know what all smart men do: The title means nothing. King or steward, it will amount to the same thing. You will be the one to rule, for the only one who might object will be in no position to stop you."

"*Mademoiselle*, you quite take my breath away," Oswald replied after a pause during which the hairs on the back of my neck stood up, even as most of the rest of it came tumbling down.

"But might I, perhaps, suggest that you have been too long away from court?" my cousin went on. "This is a place where one may think whatever one wishes, but there are still some things it is not wise to say aloud. Now, I believe I see your father trying to get your attention. Will you do me the honor of allowing me to escort you to him?"

"No, I thank you," *l'Inconnue* answered. "I am capable of crossing a room all by myself. Indeed, my whole family is considered capable . . . of many things. When you ponder the things of which it is not wise to speak, you might wish to keep that fact in mind."

"Mademoiselle," said Oswald.

I heard a sweep of skirts as *l'Inconnue* moved off. I counted to twenty, then to thirty just for good measure. "Who was that?" I asked as I came out from behind the column to stand beside my cousin. I actually had the pleasure of seeing him start, for I had genuinely surprised him.

"That is Marguerite de Renard," Oswald answered shortly.

"So that is the Fox's daughter," I said. For that is what her family's name meant. Fox. *Renard.* Though, for all of that, I'd always thought her father had a face more like a ferret than a fox. Cunning and sharp. Le Comte de Renard was a distant relation of my father's, which meant that royal blood flowed through his veins, though not enough of it to put him on the throne. Apparently, he was hoping to place his daughter there instead.

I remembered her, of course. Marguerite de Renard was just a little older than I was. She had been perfect, even as a child. And her embroidery as well. From what I could see from across the room, she had lost none of her perfection as she had grown. She had raven hair, and dark, lustrous eyes. Her face didn't look like a weasel's at all. By anyone's standards, she would be considered a beauty. I hid my stained fingers in the fold of my gown.

"I think that you should marry her," I said, and felt my cousin go very still at my side.

"Indeed, and why is that?"

"So that you may have children who are attractive and sharp-witted," I answered. "Are those not desirable attributes in the children of rulers?"

"But you forget. I will not rule here, Aurore."

"I forget nothing," I said, and was surprised to hear my voice come out like a sob. "I am not a fool just because the whole world thinks I look like one. Marguerite de Renard is right and you know it, Oswald. I thought you got resigned to being steward awfully quickly. Now I see the truth. You're only biding your time. What does it matter what you'll be called when the time comes? There will be nothing to stop you from doing whatever you like, once Papa and I are gone."

Oswald had gone white to the lips. "You think not?" he replied. "What about duty and honor, Aurore? Or don't you think I possess those attributes? No, wait. Don't answer that. Your opinion is plain enough."

By now, I was sobbing in earnest, a thing I despised but couldn't seem to stop. "I hate you. I've always hated you," I choked out. "You twist everything all around. Do what you like! Why should I care? Marry her. Don't marry her. Don't marry anyone."

At this, Oswald turned so suddenly I had no time to step away, and took my shoulders in a grip tight enough to snap my bones. "And why should I not marry her, *ma petite Aurore*? Give me one good reason. Can you do that?"

At that moment, two things happened. The musicians began to play once more. And, as if from a great distance, I heard my father's voice say:

"Aurore."

Oswald's hands fell from my shoulders as if the touch of them burned him. I stepped back, and bumped into Papa, who had come to stand directly behind me, a thing Oswald and I had been too wrapped up in ourselves to notice. Oswald brushed past us and vanished into the crowd without another word. He didn't even bow to my father.

"Aurore, what is it?" my father said, as he turned me to face him. "You're white as milk. Are you unwell?"

All of a sudden, I wished to be a child again. To

be able to crawl into his lap and rest my head against his chest to hear the way his heart beat, the thing that had always comforted me the most when I was small.

"I'm fine, Papa," I said, though suddenly I seemed to be crying harder than ever. "It's just—my shoes pinch, and my hair is a mess. I can't seem to do anything right, and I—all I want to do is go up to my room. Nobody will miss me. Please let me go up. *Please*, Papa."

"There now, that's enough. Calm yourself, Aurore," my father said, and though he did not gather me in with his arms, he did so with the look in his eyes. At this, my tears slowed, then ceased to fall altogether. "Tell me what passed between you and your cousin just now."

"No," I answered simply, and saw surprise replace the compassion in my father's eyes. This was the first time I had denied him anything, and we both knew it. And it was over Oswald. "What happened isn't Oswald's fault, it's mine. I can't think straight with all these people around, Papa. They muddle everything."

Ruin everything.

"I see," my father said. "Very well. If it is truly what you wish, you may go up to your room, Aurore. Though you will give these nobles a hold over you if you do. They have been trying to cow you all evening. If you go now, they will know that they have won."

It was either the best or the worst thing he could have said, of course. For now it meant that I must stay at the party, no matter how much my heart cried out to be alone. For there was something in it that was clambering to get out. A thing I had not known was there until now. A thing with claws, teeth, and a temper, though I still didn't know what it was called.

The musicians ended one dance and began another. My father cocked his head. "They are playing a waltz. Will you dance with me, Aurore?"

"I'll only step on your feet," I said. But I took a deep breath. *Duty and honor*, I thought. Stern and difficult taskmasters, but I must obey them both now.

"What lady wouldn't wish to dance with the most handsome man in all the room?" I went on. "And don't worry. The stains on my fingers won't rub off."

"What stains on your fingers?" asked my father.

I smiled. I'm pretty sure it was for the first time that evening. "I love you, Papa."

"And I you, Aurore. Come, let us show these overbred nobles how to dance a waltz with spirit."

"Just don't hold it against me when we fall."

At which my father laughed and plucked the few remaining pins from my hair, letting it stream down my back like a river of spun gold. I gave my head a shake, causing the river to shimmer as if struck by the sun. Then I kicked the shoes that had been making my feet miserable into the far corner of the ballroom, and let Papa lead me out into the center of the dance floor.

And so we were together when word of the first of the catastrophe was brought.

In the midst of the dance I felt a strange ripple pass through the ballroom, like an unexpected changing of the tide. A moment later, I heard a woman scream. My father spun toward the sound at once, thrusting me behind him. Before he could do anything else, the dancers parted to reveal a man dressed in the livery of the palace guards, his chest rising and falling as if he had just run a race for his life.

And his clothes . . . his clothes were covered in . . .

"Your Majesty," he gasped out. "Your Majesty, I must report—" Here his breath failed him. He collapsed to his knees and his voice choked off. At once, father knelt to support him.

"What is it?" he commanded. "Who is it that attacks us? Tell me swiftly, for God's sake, man! You are covered with blood."

At this the guard began to weep, his tears making flesh-colored rivulets down his red cheeks.

"I do not know who attacks us, Majesty," he whispered. "Or what. The blood . . . it is falling from the sky."

❧Seven❧

How shall I tell you of the days that followed, of the strange events that seemed to come upon us from all sides, threatening to tear the very fabric of our land asunder?

It rained blood for five full days, after which the sun came out but refused to go back down. Day and night it burned in the sky like a torch, till those crops that had not already drowned burst into flames in the fields where they stood. And any that survived the sun were knocked down in the hailstorm that finally put the sun's torch out, for the hailstones were as large as grown men's skulls.

Nor was that all.

Cook's favorite white cat gave birth to a red-eyed raven, then flew away with it. One of the noble's hawks hatched a litter of mice that devoured it on the spot. Wolves roamed the streets of the town at midday, their great tongues lolling from their open mouths. Flocks of larks lined the boughs of trees and sang their hearts out at deepest midnight. Stars streaked across the heavens and fell to earth. Bolts of lightning shot from clear blue skies.

The royal soothsayer was kept so busy with dire predictions that he ran out of adjectives to describe how bad things had become. And would become.

Then, as unexpectedly as they had begun, the terrible events that had plagued us stopped, and there began a series of days when nothing happened. Nothing at all.

I probably don't have to tell you that those days were the worst of all. For though things seemed normal again, none of us believed it in our hearts. We knew it for what it was. The calm before the storm that might carry us all before it.

But it is hard to do nothing when you have been doing something. You can work to put out a fire. Smother it with blankets. Carry buckets of water from the well. If it floods, you can build a dike to hold the floodwaters in check. But how do you protect yourself against an enemy you cannot see? How do you combat a thing that only threatens but never really comes?

And so it came to pass in those days of quiet that we ceased to fight an outside foe and began to fight ourselves.

It was the nobles who caused trouble first, for they had the most time on their hands and on their minds. Time to place blame and to hatch plots. And I'm sorry to say that Papa and I may have made things easier for them, for we were both away from the palace for long periods of time. For Papa saw, as the nobles could not (or would not), that it was the everyday people who were our country's true lifeblood. If they should fail, so would we all. And so he was much among them, and so was I. And so was Oswald, somewhat to my surprise, though it was impossible to predict just where or when he would turn up. Repairing buildings, furrowing and planting the fields for a second, even a third time.

It was after a day of working in the fields until my very bones ached, a day on which Oswald had not put in an appearance, cleverly, I thought, when I had the energy to think at all. At the end of such a day, Papa and I returned to the palace to find a delegation of noblemen waiting for us in the great hall. Le Comte de Renard stood at their head, so I knew there would be trouble right off.

"Your Majesty, we crave a word," le Comte said with a bow, as my father and I staggered into the hall. "The royal soothsayer has important news which you should hear at once." His eyes flicked to me, then away. "It concerns the fate of all."

Tired though he was, my father's mind was quick, much quicker than mine was. He knew, even then, I think, what was to come. "I trust you will not mind if we bathe first?" he inquired, his voice deceptively mild. "For Aurore and I have done a hard day's work while you have been communing with the stars."

At this, even le Renard had the grace to blush, and the nobles at his back dropped their eyes and shuffled their booted feet from side to side. None of them had so much as lifted a finger outside the palace, though the most virtuous and farseeing among them had gone to the aid of their estates in the countryside. But even that virtue proved to be a danger now. For it meant that the nobles left at court were the ones who cared the least for others and the most for themselves.

"We meant no disrespect," le Renard murmured. "Of course, you must refresh yourselves. Then, perhaps, we might beg a word in private?" His voice rose into the interrogative, a strange combination of demand and request combined. "We are all agreed this would be best," he said, at which the nobles stopped shuffling their feet and stood up straight, looking stern and grim. "What must be said touches upon the princess Aurore."

Beside me, I felt my father stiffen even as my own heart began to race. *Now I see*, I thought. For a terrible fear had been growing upon me, day by day, as to the cause of the dire events that had befallen us. A cause I had not yet dared to speak aloud.

"There is no need for secrecy," Papa replied. Though his voice retained its mildness all could now hear its core of solid iron. This was the voice of a king. Even in the midst of my fear, I felt a sudden surge of hope.

You have taken a false step, Monsieur le Fox, I thought. For in his dealings with others, my father hated subterfuge above all else. Even a fool could become dangerous when armed with a secret. I had heard him say this many times. Suggesting I be excluded from matters that concerned me was the worst thing le Renard could have done.

"Let the princess Aurore hear what you have to say. Pronounce what concerns her to her face. Do not whisper it behind her back like a gossipmonger," my father went on. He ran his eyes over the nobles standing at le Renard's back, and I noticed how many of them dropped their eyes.

"Furthermore, since you are all agreed, there is no need for many to deliver your message when a few will suffice. Choose those you trust the most and wait upon me in an hour."

"But, Majesty," sputtered le Renard. "Surely the princess Aurore . . ."

"Enough!" exclaimed Papa. As if they had one body, the entire group of nobles stepped back, including le Renard. "You know my will. Come prepared to speak before the princess, or do not come at all. The choice is yours. Now get out of my way."

With that, he swept by them with me scurrying along like a terrier at his side. Neither of us looked back, though I could feel my father vibrate with tension until we turned a corner and were out of sight. He did not slacken his pace until he reached my room. There, at last, he stopped. He pulled in one deep breath, scrubbed his hands across his face as if to clear his mind, then took me gently by one arm.

"Le Renard is clever, but he thinks so highly of his own cleverness he turns his strength to weakness," said my father. "Do not fear him, Aurore. But come to me as soon as you have bathed. I would have us all together before these loyal and concerned noblemen arrive."

Somewhere in the passages between the great hall and my bedroom I had begun to shake. I could not stop, no matter how I tried. But I knew that now was not the time to burden my father with my own fears, so all I said was:

"It shall be as you wish, Papa."

At this, he sighed and took my face between his hands. "Someday," he whispered. "Someday it shall be as we both might wish, Aurore. Though not, I fear, for many years yet. Until then, I pray you, remember the words your godmother spoke on the day you were christened: Keep what you hold in your heart safe and strong."

Then he turned and left me, hurrying on to the rooms he shared with Maman. No sooner had he departed than Nurse swooped down upon me, fussing and scolding over the state of my hair and clothes. Not that she wasn't prepared, of course. The water for my bath was already steaming, the great copper tub set before the fire. I was clean in next to no time.

But, no matter what I did, how many times hot water was added, how many minutes I stood before the fire to dry, I could not get warm. For my father's words and my own fears were like two cold fists clenched around my heart.

The catastrophes had returned, and this time they came from within, not from without. Bad as what we had already endured had been, I knew the worst was yet to come.

❧Eight❧

"We greatly regret that circumstances compel us to intrude upon you at this most difficult time, Majesties," purred le Comte de Renard.

He bowed low, then straightened, his glance somehow managing to linger on Maman and slide over me entirely. This, though she and I were sitting in my father's private audience chamber, side by side on the same straight-backed sofa. A piece of furniture I was usually careful to avoid because it was so incredibly uncomfortable. That night, however, anything I might do to demonstrate the strength and straightness of my spine had definitely seemed to be in order.

Le Renard had been clever to address Maman, I had to admit. She was well known to appreciate flowery words in matters of protocol. I doubted she would be swayed by them tonight, but the Fox was apparently taking no chances. *He has used his hour to regroup*, I thought.

"But when, in great agitation, the royal soothsayer came to me with what he had learned, I thought it best to bring the matter before you without delay," he went on, switching his attention to Papa who stood just beside us. "In this . . ."

"You are all agreed," my father broke in. "I know."

At this, le Renard bowed again, though I could see an angry red blush begin to creep along his cheekbones. *Don't antagonize him, Papa,* I thought. *A cornered animal is almost as dangerous as a wounded one. Did you not teach me this yourself?*

At that moment, I caught a strange, intent expression on Oswald's face out of the corner of my eye. He was standing to one side of the room, before the fireplace, a location that put him almost precisely halfway between the groups comprised of our immediate family, and that of le Comte de Renard and his allies. A position I couldn't help but notice was ambiguous at best. Though we had never spoken of it again, I was certain neither of us had forgotten what had passed between us the night of my birthday party. I had not forgotten the words of Marguerite de Renard. Was he already in league with the Fox? Did that explain his absence from the fields today?

"Duty and honor," he had said on the night of my party. Could he speak so and then betray us?

No, I thought. *Please, not Oswald.*

But when I followed the line of Oswald's eyes I discovered a curious thing. It was not le Renard he studied so intently. It was the men who stood behind him.

Select those you trust the most, my father had commanded. Apparently, they were five in number. Between them, they represented some of the most powerful families in all the land. At the very back stood the royal soothsayer, looking as if he'd rather be somewhere else. And suddenly, as if Oswald's attention had shown me the way, I saw what it was that Papa had done. He had forced le Renard to make a choice.

If the Fox brought men below him in birth, he would be proclaiming himself the clear ring-leader of whatever this was. If he brought his peers, he would be revealing his closest allies. He had chosen the second course, and had thereby given my father the advantage. For the fact that le Renard was the spokesman had already revealed his prominent place. Now my father knew the identities of his key supporters as well.

"Naturally, we must appreciate the swiftness of your actions and the depth of your concern for our daughter as well as our kingdom, Monsieur le Comte," I heard my mother say to Renard, and, at this, I pulled my attention back to the Fox himself. "Perhaps you will begin by explaining why the royal soothsayer felt unable to come to me with what he learned."

For this is what he should have done, the thing that made le Renard's actions smack of conspiracy as much as anything else. In my father's absence, it was my mother who stood for him, not le Renard. A thing the royal soothsayer, indeed, the whole kingdom, knew perfectly well.

"It was considered a matter of some delicacy, Madame," le Renard replied, and he did glance at me now. As if trying to calculate my strength, my weakness. "It was felt, perhaps, a mother's love . . ."

"Would make me blind to the needs of my country, while you and these others, having only love for country and none for my daughter, must be considered neutral?" queried Maman. "An interesting contention, Monsieur le Comte," she went on, not allowing le Renard to respond. "And one I will not soon forget. On this, you have my promise."

I saw Oswald's eyebrows raise in appreciation even as I bit back a smile. The Fox was learning that it was not so easy to sway my mother with pretty words.

"Let the soothsayer come forward," my father said. "I will hear what he has determined from his own mouth and no one else's."

There was a moment of shuffling feet, and then the group behind le Renard parted. He stepped back and the soothsayer stepped forward. He was dressed in a long black robe which concealed everything but his hands and face, making him look like some enormous and bizarre puppet. His hands were long and very white. His eyes were huge and watery. As if the years he had spent interpreting signs that no one else could even see had stretched him, pulled him out of focus.

"Well," said my father. "What is so important you must tell others before waiting for my return when you know full well where I am?"

The soothsayer's huge eyes darted from side to

side, as if seeking for a means of escape. Not finding one, they came to rest upon me as he answered:

"You must send the princess Aurore away. As far away as possible."

For an instant, no one spoke.

"Your reasons?" said my father. Not because he wanted to, of this I am certain. But because he felt he had no choice. It was a king's job to get to the bottom of things. To ask questions others would not.

"But surely the reasons must be obvious, Sire," said the soothsayer, relaxing a bit now. Perhaps he felt relieved that my father had not simply ordered his head lopped off at once for daring to suggest that the king send away his only child. Not that there had been a beheading in more years than anyone could remember. Still, a custom that has not been strictly outlawed may always be revived.

"You have only to think of the great calamities which have lately befallen our kingdom," the soothsayer went on. "The signs have shown me that they have the same root, the same cause. Furthermore, they suggest . . ."

"Are you by any chance trying to say," my cousin Oswald interrupted in a very soft voice, "that the dreadful hardships that have lately come upon us are because of the princess Aurore?"

Now a second silence filled the room, even longer than the first. *Of course that is what he is trying to say*, I thought. Someone had been bound to say it, sooner or later. It had been only a matter of time.

Had I not told myself the same thing in the dead of night, when the sleep I so desperately needed had refused to come?

"Augury is not an exact science," the soothsayer blustered, wringing his long, white hands.

"True," Oswald responded. "In fact, I think we may safely say that it is not a science at all. But surely you must have some basis for what you have come to believe."

"Of course I do," the soothsayer snapped. "My reasons come from the very events themselves. Wet contends with dry. Fire with ice. Predators give birth to prey and are devoured by it. Lightning strikes out of a cloudless sky."

"Opposites," I said, speaking aloud for the very first time. Slowly, I rose to my feet and faced the soothsayer. "You mean opposites contend, just like the spells spoken over me in my cradle. You mean that they are the root of our present calamities, and I am their cause."

"No!" Oswald said swiftly. Vehemently. "You must not say such things, Aurore."

But the soothsayer never took his eyes from my face. "I am afraid the princess is correct, my lord. For remember this, also. It was when she turned sixteen that the calamities began."

"The year the spells will be fulfilled," I said.

And the soothsayer answered: "Even so."

"Why should I send Aurore away, then?" my father asked. "Will she not simply carry calamity with her wherever she goes? Or are you suggesting I set out to conquer what few enemies I have by sending my daughter to visit them, one by one?"

"Let her at least go from the court," le Renard spoke up. "She enjoys the outdoors, does she not? Perhaps a habitation in the countryside could be found."

"A fine suggestion," Oswald put in. "I'm sure she'd enjoy your properties, my lord, particularly the ones nearest the ocean. Unless you fear she'd cause too many storms and sink all those ships of yours with their fine, rich cargoes."

"If I might suggest," the soothsayer murmured, as le Renard stepped toward Oswald, his color high. "There is another course of action we might pursue. Though I fear, Majesties, it will be even less to your liking."

At these words, a third and final silence fell upon us. A terrible silence. A silence like a blight. In it, I seemed to feel all joy within me wither, as the crops that should have grown and sustained our people had so lately done. I sank back down onto the straight-backed couch.

I knew what the soothsayer meant. We all did. If the spells spoken over me in my cradle were fulfilled, the war within me would be over. The calamaties which threatened to destroy us all would stop. All it would take was the prick of a finger. Followed by one bright drop of my life's blood.

I heard a rustle of garments as my father moved to stand behind me and my mother. Exactly between us, framed by the curve of our heads and necks as we sat upon the sofa. Connecting us, turning the three of us into one as he laid a hand on each of our shoulders. Though I could not see him, for I did not turn, I had some notion of what was in his face, for I saw it in reflected in the eyes of those who stood before us.

And the thing in my father's face was so pure and fierce that, strong though they were, the noblemen cried out and shielded their eyes, all save the soothsayer and le Renard. Oswald stood to one side as he had throughout, so still it seemed to me he had been turned to stone.

"We will speak no more of this," my father said, in a voice that I cannot to this day describe. For it contained so many things it was like a thousand voices speaking all together. A single voice and yet a chorus. "Leave me now, if you value your lives."

At this, even le Renard looked shaken. "Your Majesty, we only meant . . ."

"Oh, keep talking. Please," said Oswald.

At this, le Renard's face blanched. Without another word, he and the nobles with him bowed as if they had a single body, then backed out the audience-chamber door. As if they feared my father might yet change his mind and slay them on the spot if they turned their backs upon him. The royal soothsayer scuttled out behind them all.

"Well," Oswald said when the door was safely closed. "Something tells me that little worm will soon be looking for another job."

"You can't call him little," I contradicted, though how I managed to speak through a throat that had suddenly become so constricted I could hardly breathe I do not know. "He's way too tall."

"True. But let us both at least agree that he is low."

"Oh, how can you?" my mother exclaimed suddenly. "How can you joke at a time like this, the two of you?"

A sentiment that was somewhat undermined when my father laughed aloud. Not that he sounded all that amused.

"Let them joke, Mathilde," he told Maman. "They remind me to keep my perspective." He moved to the front of the sofa and knelt down before me, taking my hands in his, rubbing them when he found that they were cold.

"I want you to go back to your room and get a good night's sleep, Aurore. Don't let the ramblings of frightened fools keep you awake. In the morning, we will decide what must be done." Then he released me and stood. "You will see her to her room, Oswald."

"With pleasure, Uncle."

"Good night, then," said my father.

And though he turned away swiftly, he was not swift enough, for I saw the thing that was in his heart. The thing that the others had seen in his face. That had made them cry out and cover their eyes.

Grief.

For his own fate. But even more, for mine.

❧Nine❧

$\mathcal{B}$y the time Oswald and I reached my rooms, I had made up my mind. Not that I mentioned this to him, of course. Some things are best kept to yourself. Particularly when you're not sure whether or not other people will approve, but you're pretty sure they won't.

So I simply thanked him for seeing me safely to my room, went inside, then dismissed my nurse, who had waited up for me as she always did, drowsing in a chair before the fire. Though my heart hammered that I should *hurry, hurry, hurry,* for a moment I stood still in the center of my room. As if the rules of the universe had suddenly changed and the racing of my mind and heart had unexpectedly resulted in my limbs becoming frozen.

And then I realized that the reason for my paralysis was this: I had absolutely no idea what I was about to face. I only knew that, for the first time in my life, I would be all alone.

Though I might need new skills, there would be no one to teach them to me. No one of whom I could ask questions, from whom I could learn, as I had done for so long. I would have no mentors. No teachers. No one to guide me. What I was about to attempt was a thing that only I could do. And I would do it on my own.

And so, even as my mind and heart raced on ahead, my body paused, wanting one last moment in familiar surroundings before embarking into a great unknown. One last moment of solid ground before leaping straight out over a bottomless abyss. Then the moment passed, and my limbs began to obey the dictates of my heart and mind.

Near the alcove where my bed lay were two identical wooden chests, sitting side by side. The right one held what Nurse referred to as *garments befitting a princess*. Of the contents of the left chest, she preferred not to speak at all. It was this chest that I now opened, for it contained clothing much more suited for what I was about to attempt.

From this trunk, I selected a homespun shirt, a leather jerkin, and my favorite pair of breeches. Followed by warm socks and my sturdiest, most supple pair of boots. These I put on, being careful to fold the *garments befitting a princess* I was taking off and put them in their proper place. Nurse was going to be upset enough as it was. There was no sense in adding to her distress by not taking care of the things she valued.

Then I took out a second set of work clothes nearly identical to the first and put them in a knapsack I could carry upon my back, leaving both my arms free. To this, I added my knife in its sheath, though, after a moment, I took it out again and

strapped it to my right leg so that the hilt just pro-
truded above the top of my boot. I didn't know into
what kind of danger I might be going, and I could
hardly defend myself with a knife safely tucked away
in a knapsack on my back.

From the kitchens, I could acquire provisions.
From the stables, my bow and arrow, which I kept
hidden behind a bale of hay in my horse's stall so
Maman would not come to know about them. My
mind whispered that I should take the horse as well,
for I would make better time if I did. But my heart
rebelled. I had no wish to take him into unknown
danger, for I loved him well.

So I would go alone, and go on foot. Go without
further delay. Go now. *Out through the kitchen gardens*,
I thought, as I hoisted the pack upon my back, then
covered it by tossing on my warmest cloak. A thing
that seemed right and fitting, for had I not taken my
first steps into the world through the same door?

Not only that, if I went that way, I could stop at
the healer's cottage on my way to the stables. She
slept in the palace, so she would never know until
after I was gone. And taking with me what I might
need to bind a wound or treat a fever seemed a wise
and sensible thing.

If I was going to go haring off, I ought to be wise
and sensible about one thing at least.

Sucking in a breath, I blew out my candles, then
waited until my eyes had adjusted to the room being
lit by the firelight alone. The palace corridors would

be much like this as I made my way along them, illuminated by torches set at regular intervals along the walls. Earlier in the evening, they would have blazed brightly. But by now, they would have burned down low. When I was satisfied that my eyes would serve, I moved to my door and eased it open, then leaped back, startled.

Oswald stood on the other side.

Arms folded tightly across his chest as if to keep his heart from bursting out of it. His eyes hot and furious, a thing I could have discerned even had the room been much darker than it was.

"I knew it," he said. "You're going to run. You're so predictable, Aurore."

Before I quite realized what I intended, I took two steps forward, seized him by the front of his shirt, yanked him over the threshold, and closed the door behind him. How I managed not to slam it, I have no idea.

"I am not running," I hissed. "At least not running away."

"What does that mean?" he shot back, though he did keep his voice down. "That you're running *toward*? Don't be stupid. Running is running. Don't do it. You'll be giving that weasel le Renard exactly what he wants."

"So what if I am?" I said. "Even a weasel is capable of seeing the truth, Oswald. If they have nothing else, they have sharp eyes."

"And teeth," said my cousin.

"It doesn't matter! Don't you understand?" I cried. "He's right! You know it. I know it. Even Papa knows, though he doesn't want me to see that he does. All the terrible things that are happening to us—they're all my fault. They'll keep on happening as long as I stay. I have to go away. Don't try to stop me. Please, Oswald."

We stared at each another, and I realized both of us were breathing hard.

"I sincerely hate it when you do that," Oswald said at last.

"Do what?"

"Say please. Appeal to my better nature."

"It shouldn't. I'm not so sure you have one."

"Oh, Aurore." As if suddenly incredibly weary, Oswald crossed the room and sat down on the edge of my bed. After a moment, I went to sit beside him. "You really don't think very much of me, do you?"

"It's not that," I protested. "It's just—I don't understand you, Oswald. I never have. Not really."

"What's so mysterious about me?" he asked, his voice as sad as I had ever heard it. Actually, I don't think I'd ever heard Oswald sound sad before. "Why should we be so different, you and I? Do you think I don't want the same things you do?"

"To wear my father's crown, you mean," I said, and heard him draw in one swift breath.

"That really *is* what you think, isn't it?" he asked, and now his voice was bitter. "It's what you've always thought. Devious, scheming Cousin Oswald. So devious and scheming it never occurs to you I might want something simple and mundane. So simple and mundane you don't even see it when it's yours.

"What about, to be a part of a family? To be wanted. To be loved. Did you never think I might want those things, *ma petite Aurore?*"

"But," I said, then found the words I'd been about to say simply die away and slide back down my throat. For the truth was that such a thing had never occurred to me. Not even once. I don't think it had occurred to any of us, not even to Papa.

Oswald turned his head. I could feel his eyes upon my face. "You might as well just admit it," he said.

And so I told the truth and answered, "No."

He sighed, as I'd placed and lifted a great burden on his shoulders all at once.

"Wait a minute. You are part of a family," I said, sitting up a little straighter. Angry all of a sudden. "We're a family, aren't we?"

Oswald gave a derisive snort. "Don't insult my intelligence, Aurore. Having relatives isn't the same as being part of a family."

"But you never said anything," I protested. At which he snorted once again.

"What on earth would you have had me say? One cannot simply ask to be loved. To be included where one is not. 'Please pass the marmalade, Uncle, and, oh, by the way, could you see your way clear to think of me not as your brother's son but as your own?'"

"You could have tried giving it," I said.

"It isn't as simple as that, Aurore."

Now it was my turn to snort. "Don't *you* be stupid. Of course it is. How many people do you think have the courage to love all on their own? It's really much easier when you do it in groups."

"You make it sound like a herd of cows."

My lips twitched. "I prefer the image of a flock of birds, myself."

"Crows?"

"Snow geese. I'm sorry, Oswald."

To my astonishment, he closed one of his hands over mine, then raised it to his lips and pressed a kiss into my palm. Then he kept my hand in his, resting it lightly upon one knee.

"So am I, *ma petite Aurore*. I kept telling myself that, someday, one of you would see me, see the things for which my heart longed. But you never did. There were days when I thought I knew just how Cousin Jane must have felt."

"Invisible," I whispered, and felt my whole body begin to shiver as fingers of ice walked down my spine. "It's you in my dream. Not her. It's been you all along."

"What dream? What are you talking about?" asked Oswald.

"I have nightmares," I answered. "Nurse is the only one who knows."

"Nightmares," he echoed, plainly bewildered. "How long has this been going on?"

"Since I turned ten," I said. "Since I first went outside. Once a month, on the same date as my christening, I dream that I am someone else. Someone lonely and in pain, searching for a thing they treasure, but have lost. They search so long, they become invisible. No one sees them, and so no one recognizes they're the same as everybody else. They have the same desires, needs, and wants. Until the day comes when their desire changes, and being rid of the pain consumes them. This becomes the only thing they want. To do that, they're willing to do anything, even inflict great pain themselves."

"Jane. You are dreaming of Cousin Jane," said Oswald, but his voice had suddenly gone hoarse.

"So I have always thought."

"But now you're not so sure, is that it?"

"I don't know," I said. "I don't even know if it's important." At this, we both fell silent, as if trying to decide where to go next. And then I heard myself ask one of the questions to which I'd always wanted an answer. "Did you know her?"

"No," Oswald answered. He toyed absently with the fingers of my hand. "Not really. Not in the way I think you mean."

"But you saw her," I persisted. At which he nodded.

"Yes. The first time it happened, I was so young I didn't even know who she was. She scared me half to death. After that, I got used to coming across her from time to time. We rarely spoke. But seeing someone is not the same as knowing them."

"I know that."

His lips curved up, though it wasn't really a smile. "It won't do any good to run, Aurore. Your father will only come after you. Have you thought of that?"

"Yes," I said. "That's why I'm going where no one will follow: to la Forêt."

At this, Oswald dropped my hand as if my fingers scalded and shot up from the bed. "For pity's sake, Aurore!" he exclaimed. "Have you gone mad? You can't go there. You mustn't."

"It's the only way," I said. "Whatever my destiny is, it's mine and nobody else's. And I—I can't explain it, but I think that la Forêt is where I'll find it."

"Is this another one of those things that you just know?" my cousin asked.

"Something like that," I replied.

No sooner did I admit this than a great urgency seized me. My limbs became restless all at once and I stood up. As if my very bones and muscles had come to the same conclusion my mind suddenly had: If I didn't leave now, I might never have the strength of heart to try again.

I moved to stand before my cousin, gazing straight up into his face. "Promise me something, Oswald."

"What?" he asked, and though his voice was steady, I could see the turmoil in his eyes.

"Look after Papa and Maman when I am gone."

At this, a strange combination of hope and fear came into my cousin's face. "I'll do my best," he said.

"But they won't want me. They'll want you. You are going to break their hearts, Aurore."

"No," I said, my voice calm and certain. "Their hearts were broken long ago. Cousin Jane did that. They have just been waiting for the proper time to come apart."

To my amazement, Oswald reached down and gently grasped my chin, angling my face upward as if he wished to see it more clearly.

"When did you grow up?"

A second surge of urgency flooded through my veins. This time, for him.

"Tell them, Oswald. Tell them that you want them. Better yet, *show* them. Maybe you haven't been invisible your whole life. Maybe you've just been hiding."

"Oh, so now I'm a coward, is that what you're trying to say?"

"Worse. You're a scheming, devious coward."

He gave a strangled laugh and pulled me against him. "Shut up, Aurore. Any more declarations of affection like that and you'll break my heart too."

We stood for a moment with his arms around me and my head cradled against his chest. I could hear his heart beat against my ear. A different sound from the one that Papa's made, but, to my surprise, just as strong and comforting.

Seeing someone isn't the same as knowing them, I thought. And, for the first time, wondered about all I had seen but never known about my cousin.

✦ Nine ✦

"I promise to look after them," he said at last. "I can't promise that they'll love me, just that I'll love them. Or your father anyway. Your mother may present more of a challenge."

"I understand perfectly," I said against his chest. "Thank you, Cousin."

And suddenly, I knew that it was time to step away. To this day, that single step back is the hardest thing that I have ever done. I had thought leaving Papa and Maman would be the most difficult, but it wasn't. It was stepping out of Oswald's arms.

"There's just one more thing," I said as I stepped back.

"You're awfully full of demands, all of a sudden," Oswald said. His tone was light. But I could see the way his hands clenched and unclenched at his sides. "What must I promise this time?"

"Promise me you will never marry Marguerite de Renard," I said.

I just had time to see his mouth fall open before I spun around and sprinted for the door. I had one foot across the threshold before I heard his answer.

"I promise. Fare you well, my little cousin. I will wait for you, Aurore."

❧ Ten ❧

*A*nd so I began my journey to la Forêt.

I traveled all that night, walking swiftly. I walked on the roads when they would take me where I needed to go. When they would not, I walked across the open fields or whatever else lay before me. There were no signposts, but then I needed none. The call of the Forest itself was all I needed to guide me.

I reached it just at dawn, stomach rumbling, legs aching. I came to a halt at the place where the grass ended. A strange patch of barren earth edged the Forest on what I assumed was all four sides, for it extended in either direction as far as my eyes could see. My toes extended out past the edge of the grass as if over a bottomless pit.

Just half a dozen more steps, I thought. That's how many it would take to cross the patch of ground that marked the transition between the world of la Forêt and the world in which I'd grown up. The world comprised of everything I knew and loved. Six little steps to leave it all behind and enter who knew precisely what.

As I stood, hesitating, the sun came over the horizon with an exuberant leap. And, as the light struck the trees, it seemed to me that the Forest came to life. Branches trembled and swayed upward, as if taking a morning stretch. Trunks gleamed like polished mother of pearl in the soft, early light. In that moment, it seemed to me that I could actually see the magic of the place, shimmering like a soap bubble over the tops of the trees.

You can do it. It's only six steps, I thought. *You've come so far, you can't stop now, Aurore.*

My body refused to cooperate and remained motionless.

The sun inched higher and now it seemed to me that the trees began to converse with one another. Each leaned over to its neighbor, first on the right, then on the left, in a great rippling motion, as if passing some vital piece of information from tree to tree in a great chain of knowledge that would soon be spread throughout the Forest. Then, as I watched, trees in the foremost line waved their branches in my direction, the very leaves curling forward, then back, as if beckoning me in.

I felt a breath of air pass over my face and, in that moment, I knew what it was the trees of la Forêt whispered to one another.

Aurore.

Aurore, they said. *Welcome. We have been waiting for you.*

At this I might not have been able to move at all, had not an unusual thing happened at almost the very same moment. A great gust of wind struck me from behind, strong as a hand in the small of my back. One. Two. Three. Four. Five steps I stumbled forward before I regained control of my limbs and brought myself to a teetering halt. Now I stood so close to la Forêt I could almost hear it breathing. One more step, and I would be beneath its boughs.

Now there was no wind at all, as if, instinctively, the Forest knew the same thing I did—that this final step must come from me, and me alone. It must be my will that carried me forward and no other's. For only then would I truly have chosen my own destiny, embraced no matter my misgivings, whatever it was that la Forêt might hold in store.

I pulled in five deep breaths. On the sixth, I took the final step. And so the deed was done.

How shall I tell you what going into la Forêt was like? Though I moved through the air, passing beneath the trees for the first time felt exactly the same as wading in a pool of deep, clear water. As if the magic of the place had given the air a texture and substance it did not possess in the world outside. It pushed against me as I moved through it, as if in silent challenge. Then, over my head, I heard the branches begin to stir once again.

Aurore, they said. *Aurore. At last. We've been waiting for so long.*

At that, I made a decision. We had to come to some sort of arrangement, the Forest and I. I couldn't let things continue as they were, with la Forêt being magical and mysterious and my heart beating just a little bit too hard.

"I hear you," I said, deciding my best course of action would be to speak out boldly, beginning as I wanted to be able to go on, even if that was the opposite of what I actually felt like doing. "I do have ears." To demonstrate, I pushed the curtain of my hair aside. "I'm sure I'm very sorry to have kept you waiting, though I had no idea that I was doing it. If there's something you want me to know or do, you might as well just come right out with it. Being all mysterious will only make me cross, which neither of us will like."

At this, a gust of wind swept through the branches like a sudden laugh and blew into my face with such force that I threw a hand up to cover my eyes. When I brought it down again, la Forêt was quiet and still. Even more, the air was now the consistency of which I was accustomed, though it was so clear and pure it brought tears to my eyes.

Now I could see that the trees, which from outside the Forest had pretty much all looked alike, were in fact as different from one another as people are. Some were smooth-barked; others had rough skins. They had shades ranging from the black of ebony, to the red of cherry, to the papery-white of ash and alder. The air was so clear that I could see from many feet away a thin line of black ants marching in single file up the burnished copper bark of a madrona.

The everyday rules regarding the habitats of trees did not seem to exist inside of la Forêt. Spruce and figs grew side by side, embracing one another. *It is a study in opposites,* I thought. *Just as I am.* And I heard the Forest sigh and rustle. As if a question that had troubled it had been answered, and a course of action decided upon. And that was the moment I lost what remained of my fear, or most of it, for it seemed to me that la Forêt had reached our agreement, even if I didn't yet understand quite what it was.

Naturally, no sooner did I have this encouraging thought than overhead there broke out the loudest clap of thunder I had ever heard and it began to storm. To hail, to be precise. And though the hailstones were only as large as a grown man's fist, and not his skull, they were more than large enough to make me scurry for shelter.

The first place I tried was beneath the boughs of the biggest evergreen I could find. But the wind gave it a mighty shake, causing all the hailstones that had been trapped among the branches to rain down upon my head at once. Next I tried crawling beneath some low-growing shrub, only to be chased off by a fox who had taken shelter there along with her cubs. Finally I tried clambering up into the branches of the madrona, but instead slid right down its smooth copper trunk.

At that, I gave up.

"Must we play twenty hiding places?" I shouted at the storm. "Three is more than enough. I can take a hint. I'm not stupid. Just show me where you want me to go."

As if in answer, the wind snatched at my cloak,

tugging until I turned around. Through the driving hail, I could just make out the outline of a cottage, a thing I had somehow failed to notice before. This so surprised me I was incapable of moving for several moments, completely oblivious to the fact that I was growing colder and wetter with every second.

How could there be a cottage in la Forêt when it had been forbidden to go there for time out of mind? It wasn't until a hailstone hit me on the head that I found my legs. Questions could be answered later. Right now, I needed to get out of the storm.

I dashed madly for the cottage, the wind pushing from behind. By the time I reached it, my hands were so cold and wet I couldn't work the latch, so I ended up kicking at the door. I was just on the point of raising my leg to try to kick it in when it opened. I lost my balance and somersaulted across the threshold, landing in a great puddle of water and mud in the middle of the floor.

"I believe it's customary to knock before you kick the door in," a voice said.

Then the door slammed behind me and I was staring up into the face of a young man I had never seen before.

❖Eleven❖

His eyes were the same color as the branches of the evergreens, and were flecked with gold in a way that reminded me instantly of Oswald. Looking up into them was like gazing up into the Forest's canopy with the sun dappling down. His hair was muddy brown. He looked exasperated with me, to say the least.

"I didn't think anyone was here," I gasped. "I didn't think people lived in la Forêt. If I've hurt your home, I'm sorry."

"Yes, well," he said after a moment. He leaned back and stopped looming over me. "I suppose your haste was understandable. The storm really *is* remarkable. I've never seen such hailstones, have you?"

At this, he scurried to one of the windows and began to peer out, his irritation with me apparently completely forgotten. The look on his face was such a strange combination of studiousness and excitement, I half expected him to start making notes. A moment later, to my amazement, he pulled a quill, ink, and a small leather-bound book out of a knapsack at his feet, and did just that, not noticing when he dripped ink down the front of his shirt.

I had seen such hailstones, of course, and ones that were even larger. But since my unexpected companion seemed so excited about the size of the ones currently hurtling through the trees and thundering on the roof, I decided to keep quiet about it. At least one of us was enjoying the current situation. It seemed a shame to spoil it.

"Oh, and by the way, I don't live here," he went on. He made a notation in his book, then pressed his nose against the glass. I feared he'd decide to open the window in another moment. "This isn't my home. I've come to the Forest on a great quest."

He spoke those last two words as if they should be spelled entirely with capital letters, punctuating them by shutting his book with a snap. I tried in vain to think of a suitable reply.

"That's nice," I finally said.

He turned back then, his expression slightly crestfallen, and I realized he'd probably expected me to ask him what it was. A thing I most likely would have done, if I hadn't suddenly been feeling so out of sorts. It had taken all the courage I possessed to enter la Forêt, or at the very least, a whole lot of courage. While I hadn't been sure what to expect, I *had* expected to face it on my own. I might even have been looking forward to it, in a funny sort of way. A test of my inner strength, or something like that. Of my ability to be brave, to do what was right, even if that meant hardship and sacrifice.

Now here I was, in a cottage that shouldn't be

there, with a companion who viewed a hailstorm as an opportunity for note-taking, claimed to be on a great quest, and yet somehow managed to look as if he might have trouble pulling on his boots in the morning. Not at all what I'd expected, to say the least.

Oh, for heaven's sake, Aurore, I chastised myself as I climbed soggily to my feet. *Oswald is right about you. You really are the most contrary girl alive. Anybody else would be happy to have discovered they're not alone, but not you. No, you're actually feeling cross because you haven't ended up all by yourself.*

"I don't suppose you're any good at fire building, are you?" the young man inquired suddenly. I realized then that, in spite of his enthusiasm for the hail, he was just as wet as I was.

"I did my best, but the truth is, I'm not very good at practical things. My hands never seem to know what to do, no matter how often they've been told how. I'm much more of a scholar, really." He attempted a cajoling smile. "You know, brains over brawn?"

"As long as my flint didn't get wet," I answered, and I unfastened my cloak and shook it out. It was heavy with water, but it had done its work well, for beneath it my knapsack was dry. I hung the cloak on a peg near the door, then turned, hands on hips, to take stock of the cottage.

Whoever had built it had definitely known what they were doing. The roof didn't leak. The fireplace stood in the cottage's very center, so that all the heat it generated would be trapped inside. I could see firewood stacked neatly to one side of the hearth, with a basket of kindling nearby.

"Someone must live here," I said finally. "It's too well kept to have been abandoned."

"I've been thinking the same thing." The young man nodded. "I hope whoever lives here isn't getting too wet."

"And that they don't mind that we came here to get dry. Well, let's see what I can do." I moved toward the fireplace, then stopped. Resting in front of it was something I hadn't noticed before. A sickly green rug with bumps as big as the coils of giant snakes.

"You'll want to keep an eye on that rug," my companion advised. "I walked across it when I first got here and it almost pitched me flat on my face. It seems to have a mind of its own."

But that's not possible, I thought. I knew where this rug was, or at least I knew where it belonged. Papa kept it in his study. I'd made it for him as a birthday gift shortly after I'd turned nine.

"Thanks for the warning," I said.

Carefully, I lifted the rug and moved it to one side. No doubt there was an explanation for its presence here, but it wouldn't do much good to think about it. I was unlikely to figure out what it was. Instead I concentrated on fire-building, a thing I was good at. The wood was well seasoned. It caught at once, and I soon had a bright blaze going.

"Oh, well done!" the young man exclaimed, and he

put away his writing supplies and knelt down at my side. We stayed that way for a moment, both of us warming our hands. If it bothered him that it had taken me so little time to perform a task he'd claimed had defeated him, he didn't let it show. I could feel my irritation begin to fade away. It's hard to be cross with someone who isn't cross back, particularly when you're safe and warm in the bargain.

"What's your name?" I asked.

To my surprise, he reddened, as if my everyday question was cause for embarrassment. "I was afraid you were going to ask me that," he said. "Sooner or later, every new person I meet does. I don't suppose you'd like to take three guesses and choose the one you like the best?" He must have seen the astonished look on my face, because almost at once he said: "No, I didn't think so. Very well, if you must know, I'm called Prince Ironheart."

"What's wrong with that?" I asked. "It's a fine name. Strong and true."

"Yes, well, I'm afraid it's also something of a joke," he confessed. "I was dubbed that by my older brother in a moment of extreme annoyance. I mentioned I'm not very clever with my hands, didn't I? The truth is, I'm often downright clumsy. I once managed to drop his favorite sword in a way that caused it to splinter into exactly seven shards, after which it took the same number of days to put it back together again. As a matter of fact . . ."

He settled down cross-legged on the floor and

his tone grew hushed and confidential, as if he was preparing to tell me a bedtime story.

"It was really quite a remarkable feat, if you stop to think about it. The royal mathematician and I did some computations later, and discovered that the odds against such a thing occurring were well over one in a hundred thousand. But it was after this that my brother started calling me Ironheart. He said my heart would have to be strong, since my arms so obviously aren't."

All of a sudden, I discovered I was liking Ironheart quite a bit better than I'd expected to, a thing I'm pretty sure had to do with a feeling of kinship inspired by the word *clumsy*.

"What's his name?" I asked. "Prince Smartmouth?"

"No," Ironheart answered, his tone slightly troubled. "Actually, it's Prince Valiant. It suits him, which makes it even worse."

I settled down cross-legged myself and gave his knee a reassuring pat. "I don't think I like him."

"Oh, but you would," protested Ironheart. "Everybody does, except, perhaps, for Grandfather. Just between you and me, Grand-père thinks that Valiant is something of a prig. He told me so on the eighth day. You know—the one on which the incident with the sword could finally be considered over."

I laughed, my earlier irritation with his presence now completely forgotten. "I *know* I like your grandfather. But surely you must have a given name. A birth or christening name that you could use instead."

"Of course I do," he said. "It's Charles. But somehow, Ironheart just seemed to stick. I've grown so accustomed to it, if you called me Charles I'd probably look over my shoulder to see who was behind me."

"Well, I only have one name," I said. "And it's Aurore."

His expression brightened. "I wondered if it would be that. Or something like it. The second you took your cloak off, I was reminded of the sun coming up. And Aurore means *of the dawn* doesn't it? I think it must be your hair. All that gold."

"You're right," I answered, resisting an impulse to pull my fingers through it to see if there were any snarls. It hadn't occurred to me until that moment to think about the way I looked. "Without it, I would have ended up named for my grandmother."

"What was her name?"

"Henriette-Hortense."

"Oh dear," Ironheart said involuntarily, then blushed. "That was rude, I'm sorry."

"Don't be," I said. "I agree entirely."

"Still," he said after a moment. "Even Henriette-Hortense is a proper name, not a joke like Ironheart. It's awful to know people are laughing at you, day in and day out."

Once again, he reminded me of Oswald. That was how his nickname of Prince Charming had gotten started, before he'd decided to make it his own.

"Why don't you make it true?" I asked. "Live up to your nickname and put them all to shame. *Become* Ironheart."

"How on earth would I do that?"

"You're the one with the big brain," I said. "Can't you figure something out?"

"I suppose I could," he said, though now his voice was doubtful. "I hadn't really considered that approach before. I'll have to think about it."

"What about this quest of yours? That should offer plenty of opportunities, don't you think?"

"You're right!" he exclaimed. "You're absolutely right! I wonder . . ." He broke off, his expression thoughtful.

"What is the quest, anyway?" I said, then had a terrible thought. "Not slaying a dragon, I hope."

"Oh, no," Ironheart replied at once. "Nothing like that." He paused. "Or, at least, I don't think so. There aren't a lot of details to go on, other than the basic ones. I mean, nobody knows much about the Forest, so there are a lot of unknowns."

"The quest," I prompted.

"Oh, yes. Well, it's really quite simple," he replied. "There's a beautiful princess sleeping in the heart of the Forest. I'm going to find her and wake her up."

❧Twelve❧

$\mathcal{I}$t was a good thing I was already sitting down, because if I hadn't been, I'd have probably fallen over.

"*What?*"

"'There's a beautiful princess sleeping in the heart of the forest," Ironheart repeated obligingly. "I'm going to find her and wake her up."

"With what? The kiss of true love?"

Ironheart's green eyes grew enormous. "Wait a minute," he said. "How did you know?"

I put my head down in my hands. *This can't be happening. It just can't be,* I thought. Somehow, some version of my story had gotten all mixed up. Turned around. In fact, it had gotten so confused that I was actually in the same room with someone who wanted to come and rescue me from something that hadn't even happened yet.

Just breathe deeply, Aurore, I told myself. *Calm down. He can't be talking about you. He said the princess was beautiful, or had you forgotten? That would certainly seem to rule you out.* Nobody thought that I was beautiful, with the possible exception of Nurse and Papa. Perhaps the other countries bordering la Forêt had their own tales to account for its strangeness.

"How do *you* know?" I asked.

Confusion flickered across Ironheart's face. "How do I know what?"

"How do you know there's a beautiful princess sleeping in the heart of the Forest?"

His expression cleared at once. "Oh, that. That's easy. Because Grand-père told me so. He's been telling me stories about her for as long as I can remember."

"Well how does *he* know, then?" I persisted. "How can he be so sure she's there? Has he seen her for himself?"

"Of course not!" Ironheart exclaimed. "Nobody goes into the Forest. It's been forbidden for time out of mind."

This was getting worse by the minute. "But—," I began.

Ironheart held up a hand, and I fell silent. "Do you know anyone you always believe?" he inquired. "Someone you trust with your heart, even though your mind occasionally warns you they might be pulling your leg?"

"I do, in fact," I replied, thinking once again of Oswald.

"Well, there you have it. That's what Grand-père is like. I don't know how he knows the story of the Sleeping Beauty. I just know I believe that he does."

He gazed into the fire for a moment.

"She's been sleeping in the heart of the forest almost forever. Longer than the memory of any man alive, save his, says Grandfather. All that time, she's been waiting for someone to come along and bring her true love's kiss.

"Grand-père says that many men have tried to find the Sleeping Beauty, and all have failed. He says this is because they're like my brother Valiant. Handsome, strong, and brave, even reasonably intelligent. But nothing special. Nothing out of the ordinary. But Grand-père says the princess who sleeps in the heart of the Forest is so special she could never love an ordinary man. Therefore, the one who awakens her with must be someone special also."

"And your grandfather thinks you're the one," I said.

"Actually," Ironheart confessed. "He's not my grandfather. He's my great-grandfather. Or maybe it's great-great. I can never remember. He really *is* incredibly old."

"But he's certain you're the one to break the spell," I insisted, at which Ironheart made a face.

"It is kind of far-fetched, isn't it? You don't have to tell me. I know."

"I didn't mean that."

"Well, I wouldn't blame you if you had," he said, his tone philosophical. "I know I'm not like most other princes. I've always known it. But Grand-père says that's what makes me the right one for this quest. He says being different is my strong point."

"What do you think?"

He fell silent again, gazing into the fire. While he was busy saying nothing, I busied myself watching the way the light played across his face. It was a good face, better than I'd originally given it credit for. Ordinary at first glance, but on second glance, far from ordinary.

On second glance, you noticed the stubbornness of the chin—a contrast to a mouth that, even when straight and serious, looked as if it was just waiting for its chance to smile. The cheekbones were determined, high and wide, but there was just a hint of sadness around those evergreen eyes. A face shaped by both love and adversity, I thought. But where neither held sway. They were balanced, point to point.

Once more, I was reminded of Oswald. For it came to me suddenly that this was how he might have looked, had his life contained the bedrocks I'd so recently learned he thought they lacked: Compassion. Acceptance. Love.

"I think I must believe I'm different," Ironheart said at last. "That I can be the one to break the spell. I've never really wanted to be like my brother, much as I love him. At the very least, I must want to find out whether or not what Grand-père says is true. Otherwise, I wouldn't have come."

"That's a good answer," I said. At which he looked at me and smiled.

"And that's a very nice answer. Thank you, Aurore. But what about you? What brings you to the Forest?"

I hesitated, suddenly fearful that he would think me a coward. "I guess you could say that I ran away from home."

"Oh," he said, and I could sense him hesitating, trying to decide whether or not to say more. "That must have been a difficult decision," he continued after a moment. "You don't strike me as someone who runs from her problems."

"I'm not, or at least not under ordinary circumstances," I said, more than a little grateful that this was his response. "But the circumstances were far from ordinary, so I did what I thought was best."

"In that case, I'm sure it was," said Ironheart. "What will you do now?"

I opened my mouth to answer, then closed it again. The truth, which I didn't particularly care to admit, was that I simply didn't know. Just getting to la Forêt had seemed so huge, I hadn't really thought much about what would happen after I arrived. I guess I thought it would become obvious once I got here.

"I'm not sure," I said at last. "At the time I set out, just getting here seemed like enough."

"Why don't you come with me?"

For one dazzling moment, I actually considered it. Now that I'd gotten used to his presence, I had to admit it was nice not to be alone. But I knew I couldn't do it. I had no idea what I would encounter in la Forêt. What fulfilling my destiny truly held in store. How could I go with Ironheart, possibly put him in great danger, when I hadn't even been willing to bring my horse along?

"I thought a quest was a thing you had to do by yourself," I hedged, not quite ready to say *no* outright.

"Not necessarily," he said. "Jason had the Argonauts."

"I'm not so sure that's such a great example," I commented. "Considering the way things turned out."

"Well—" He pondered for a moment, and suddenly I could see the lines of mischief deepen on either side of his mouth. "Hercules had the Labors."

I gave a snort of laughter. He was clever, I had to admit. "That's not the same thing and you know it."

"Well if you don't want to go you can just say so," Ironheart said, his tone growing offended. "Believe me, I've heard the word *no* before."

"I didn't say *no*," I said. "I just didn't say *yes*, either. And stop trying to twist my words around and confuse me and trick me into going."

"I don't trick," he replied, his voice huffy. "I wheedle and cajole. Occasionally I manipulate, but I'm always very sneaky about it, so you wouldn't know it was happening until it was far too late."

In spite of myself, my lips twitched. "Thanks for the warning."

"Not at all."

We stared into the fire for a moment.

"I ran away because things were happening," I finally said quietly. "Horrible things, calamitous things. Things which could—would—have destroyed everything I loved. They were all my fault, all because of me. Coming to la Forêt was the only way I could think of to make them stop."

"I probably shouldn't say this," Ironheart said. "But don't you think that's a bit egotistical, Aurore? In my experience, things happen for reasons, that's true enough. But very few of them actually have to do with us even when we feel as if they do."

"You don't know anything about me!" I cried. "There are things inside me, Ironheart—spells. Cast upon me from almost the moment of my birth. One dark, the other light. One seeking my destruction, the other my salvation. They're the things that almost tore my people apart."

"And you as well, I think," Ironheart said quietly. "But the fact that you carry them inside you doesn't mean they *are* you, Aurore. Or that you're responsible for them."

"What difference does that make?" I asked, suddenly as tired as I could ever remember being. "I carry them with me wherever I go. That makes them mine."

"A great deal, I should think," he answered. "Do you have no will of your own? You say you know what the spells want—your destruction or your salvation. But what about what *you* want, Aurore?"

"I don't know what I want," I whispered, for suddenly, horribly, I realized it was true. "I don't know. I have never known."

"Then come with me until you do," he said simply. "Let the journey be a quest for us both."

All of a sudden, I wanted to say *yes*. Wanted it so much, I feared to say it, lest it be the same as taking the coward's way out.

"Let me sleep on it," I said. "I'll give you my answer in the morning."

"Fair enough."

At that, Ironheart got to his feet. "I don't know about you, but I'm starving. I do have food. Grand-père supervised my packing."

"Why didn't you just bring him along?"

"I would have," Ironheart acknowledged cheerfully as he retrieved his knapsack from beneath the window and carried it to the cottage's only table. "But he said he was too old. And furthermore that going into the Forest was my destiny, while his was to wait as he had always done. He said he'd been doing it so long he'd pretty much perfected the technique."

There was a pause. "I'll bet it drives your brother crazy when you do that," I finally said.

"When I do what?" he asked, but I could see the smile lurking around his mouth like a cat after a bird.

"Refuse to take offense when one is offered." I got to my feet, pulled my knife from its sheath, then strolled to the table and picked up a loaf of bread. Holding it against my chest, I began to slice. "I'm surprised he didn't name you Ironwill."

He began to hack at a hunk of cheese. "I suppose he might have, if it hadn't already been taken. That's what the people call Grand-père, because he's lived so long. They say it's his will alone that's kept him alive for all these years. You'd like him, Aurore. He teases the same way you do, and he's quick-witted, just like you are."

"Don't," I said, as I finished slicing the bread and set down the loaf. "I said I'd think about it and I will. There's no need to wheedle. I keep my word."

"That was not a wheedle. It was an observation," said Ironheart. "When I wheedle, my voice gets kind of high and whiney. It's impossible to mistake a wheedle for anything else."

By now I was trying so hard not to laugh it was making my stomach hurt. It felt good, I realized suddenly.

"Are you always this impossible?"

Ironheart nodded cheerfully. "Almost always. It's better when I'm asleep. Unless I snore."

"You snore and I'm stuffing your cloak in your mouth."

He grinned. I grinned back. And suddenly, it came to me that I did know what I wanted, or at least a part of it. At least for now. I wanted more moments like this. Wanted a thing I had never really had, but hadn't missed until now.

A friend.

Even so, it wasn't until the middle of the night that I well and truly made up my mind. The hail had turned to a steady drumming of rain upon the roof not long after we'd eaten our cold supper, stirred up the fire, and spread our cloaks before it to dry. Then we'd parcelled out the blankets from the bed. I stayed in it, while Ironheart settled with his back to the fireplace.

But in spite of the weariness which seemed to

come from nowhere, rising up to fill me like liquid in a cup, I could not sleep. The uncertainty of the next day had cast a pall over my rest. And not me alone, for, time and again, I heard Ironheart stir at his place by the fire.

"How did you know?" I said at last. I couldn't see him where he lay on the far side of the fireplace, and so I spoke to the embers' glow. "How did you know that this quest was the right thing to do?"

He answered at once, and I could tell by his voice that he'd been pondering this very question for a very long time. "It's hard to explain," he said, his voice as quiet as mine. "I guess because, even more than Grand-père's words, I felt the truth of it inside me. I hate to sound all epic and swashbuckling, but this is what I was meant to do. It's the thing that I was born for, Aurore."

I felt my whole body relax then, the tension and uncertainty streaming out of it. Hadn't I described my desire to discover life outside the palace walls in exactly the same way? And wasn't it that same desire which, for better or worse, had brought me here, to Ironheart and la Forêt?

Who was to say going with him wasn't my destiny, just as his had been to ask me? That our destinies weren't entwined?

"All right," I said. "I'll go."

"I'm glad," he answered.

After that, we both slept peacefully for the rest of the night and dreamed of nothing at all.

❖Thirteen❖

After the storm, it had turned cold during the night. So cold that the entire Forest seemed covered in a single sheet of ice when we opened the door of the cottage the next morning. It shimmered in the morning sun like spun sugar on a child's birthday cake, snapping and crackling as we walked upon it. Even the leaves and branches were covered in a thin sheet of ice. Throughout la Forêt, nothing stirred. There was not a single sound, save for the ones Ironheart and I made ourselves.

After breakfasting, we tidied the cottage, determined to leave it as much as we had found it as possible. Ironheart folded blankets while I swept the hearth and brought in fresh wood for the fire. I still hadn't solved the mystery of the hearth rug, but I had resolved not to think about it. We shouldered our packs, put on our cloaks, and stepped out the front door, closing it firmly behind us.

"How will we know which way to go?" Ironheart asked.

"That's easy enough," I said. "We continue on past the cottage."

"How do you know ?"

"It only stands to reason," I said, as I began to circle

around to the right of the cottage. The crunch of ice beneath my feet sounded like broken panes of glass. "I came upon it not long after I'd entered la Forêt. Therefore, the cottage must be on its outskirts and the heart of the Forest must be beyond it. That means, this way."

"Um . . . Aurore?"

I was squinting straight ahead, trying to see through the sudden dazzle of the sun. "What?"

"You might want to—that is, I hate to contradict you, but—"

I brushed tears from my cheeks. The glare had become so great, it was making my eyes water. "*What?*" I said again.

In answer, Ironheart simply stopped walking. And that was when I realized that we hadn't moved at all. Or that the cottage had moved right along with us, which would perhaps be a more precise way of describing it. For in spite of the fact that we'd taken enough steps to carry us clear along one side, as soon as I stopped walking too, I found myself standing by the front door. Right where we'd started. Instantly, the glare decreased, as if to reward us.

"Oh," I said. "Well, this is annoying."

"Do you think so?" Ironheart asked. He had that look on his face, the same as the one he'd worn when staring at the hailstones, or describing the calculations he'd made concerning his brother's broken-in-seven-pieces sword. I expected the notebook to come out of the knapsack at any second.

"When you stop to think about it, it's really quite fascinating. In fact, I think the odds might be somewhere around—"

The expression on my own face must have shown my frustration because he broke off abruptly, then added. "Though it is very inconvenient, of course."

"It's just that I don't care very much for games," I said, moving straight out from the cottage by several steps in what I considered to be the wrong direction. "Too sneaky. I much prefer it when things are straightforward. They don't have to be simple or easy, but they do have to be fair."

I put my hands on my hips and glared at the closest stand of trees. *"Are you listening to me?"* I shouted.

"Maybe we should just go back inside and rest for a day," Ironheart said, his tone a bit nervous now. "You don't seem to be feeling quite yourself, Aurore."

"I feel just fine," I answered. "This will all make sense in a minute." I took a few more steps. I was under the closest branches now.

"I know you're enchanted," I shouted up at the trees. "He knows it. I know it. We all know it, so you can just stop showing off. If you want us to go in a direction that doesn't make sense to anyone but you, that's fine. You're making all the rules, anyway. That's obvious. Though I could wish I didn't feel quite so much as if you were making them up as you went along."

No sooner had I uttered these words than a bright shaft of sunlight shot through the Forest canopy to illuminate the trees under which I was standing. It was a stand of aspens, their leaves as yellow as my hair. Their trunks stood close together, the branches entwined, as if the trees had stepped closer together during the long, cold night in an effort to keep warm. Their leaves were frozen solid.

I was pretty certain this particular group of trees hadn't been there the night before, though I suppose it is possible that I just didn't notice them in the storm.

Then the sun struck the leaves, and the shimmer of ice became a sparkle, and the sparkle became a shine. And then the shine became a dazzle so bright it hurt to look upon it. And that was the moment that the leaves burst forth like hundreds of yellow butterflies all breaking free of their cocoons at the same time. They fluttered in a breeze that was for them and them alone, for though I stood beneath the boughs, I felt no breath of air.

"Looks like we're going this way," I said. The way that made no sense at all. The one I would have sworn was back the way I had originally come. But it was plainly what the Forest wanted, and equally plain I was in no position to argue.

"Whatever you say," said Ironheart.

We walked for several hours as the Forest thawed and came to life around us. I probably don't need to tell you that the direction in which we traveled was the right one after all. About the time when the trees cast no shadows because the sun was directly overhead and the day was now very warm, we came to a stream and sat down beside it to rest our legs and eat our lunch.

Ironheart ate with great determination, though I could tell his mind wasn't on the meal. He shifted restlessly every few seconds, gazing around him, a furrow between his brows.

"What's the matter?" I finally asked. "Are you sitting on an anthill?"

"It doesn't make any sense," he announced.

I'm afraid I gave a very unprincesslike snort. "You aren't just *now* figuring that out are you?"

"I mean the stream," he said. "It doesn't make any sense. There aren't any streams flowing out of the Forest, at least not where I come from. Or into it, either."

"Nor where I come from," I said. "Maybe it's just inside of la Forêt."

"But that's the thing that doesn't make any sense," Ironheart said at once. "It's not the way things are supposed to work. A stream has to start someplace and go somewhere."

"I'm sure it does," I said. "It just does it all within the boundaries of the Forest."

"But—," Ironheart began.

"The stream makes as much sense as going the wrong direction to get where we're going," I interrupted.

"You have a point," he said after a moment. He eyed the stream, *that* expression on his face again. "I wonder what it tastes like."

"I'm not so sure that's a good idea," I said. "What if it's enchanted or something?"

At this, he gave a snort of his own. "It would have to be, wouldn't it? We're in an enchanted forest."

"You know what I mean," I said.

"Of course. But we're breathing the air already. We don't have much choice about that. How much more dangerous could it be to drink the water?"

"I don't know. That's the point."

I could tell the second he made up his mind. His face took on a look of determination and his chin jutted out. "I'm doing it," he said. "Don't try to stop me, Aurore."

"Why on earth would I do that?" I inquired. "You can make up your own mind. Just don't expect me to come and rescue you if you fall into a stupor or something. I have no intention of getting all wet, and besides, that water looks cold."

He clambered down the bank of the stream and lay on his stomach atop a large stone at its edge. Then he leaned out over the stream, dipped his cupped hands into the water, and brought them up to his mouth. Drops trickled through his fingers, sparkling bright and clear as stars.

"Well?" I called.

"It's good!" he said, rolling over onto his back. "You were right. It is very cold. But there's something else. A thing I've never tasted before. I'm not quite sure how to describe it."

"Stop trying to cajole me into tasting it myself," I said.

"That wasn't cajoling," he answered, pushing himself up onto his elbows. "That was tantalizing. There's a big difference. Couldn't you tell?"

"Either way, it's not going to work."

One eyebrow shot up. "You just keep right on thinking that, Aurore."

"That's not going to work either," I said, though, by this time, I'd started to laugh, which was just as good as admitting that he'd won. "Oh, all right," I said, getting up and marching down the bank to flop down at his side. I followed his example, gathering the stream water into my cupped hands to drink. I don't think I've ever felt anything so cold. But it slid down my throat as smoothly as honey.

"Oh," I said, after a moment. And then again, "Oh."

"That just what I thought." Ironheart nodded. "It's like—"

"Like drinking from all the streams there ever were at once," I said, rolling over to gaze up at the sky. Like being able to hold the clear, pure essence of the very world itself within your hands, and then take it in with one long swallow. "I wonder if that's how the magic of this place works."

Ironheart sat up. "What?"

"Doesn't it seem to you that there's more of everything here?" I asked, sitting up also. "As if the Forest holds all the possibilities for everything all at once? Maybe that's why time is different here."

He was nodding vigorously even before I finished

speaking. "That's exactly how it seems to me," he said. "But what I wonder is this: Do we choose what we experience here, or does the Forest choose it for us?"

"My guess is that it's both," I answered slowly. "It definitely guided me to the cottage last night. And this morning, it wouldn't let us go in the direction we wanted. But since then, it's pretty much left us alone."

"I wonder why it cares where we go," Ironheart said. The frown was back between his eyes. "And whether it's taking us toward its heart or away from it."

"There's only one way to find out," I said. At which he nodded and got to his feet.

"Let's go."

❧Fourteen❧

We walked for days, generally going the way the Forest wanted us to go. Any time we tried to turn around, or choose an alternate path, the same thing happened as at the cottage: We ended up right back where we'd started. Finally, even I gave up trying to go do anything but travel in the direction the Forest wished. We could do nothing but trust the steps we took would bring us closer to our goal.

One day the trees through which we walked were comprised entirely of evergreens—pine and fir. The pine bows were heavy with fat, brown cones. Now and again, one would fall from its branch and land with a *thunk* upon the long needles that covered the floor of the Forest like a great green rug, never turning brown themselves at all. Delighted, as if the Forest had offered him a gift, Ironheart stuffed several of the cones into his knapsack, taking them out to sketch and make notations whenever we stopped.

There was the day we walked through an orchard of saplings so energetic we could actually see them grow. It was on this day that Ironheart stopped putting his quill, ink, and leather-bound book away in his knapsack. Instead he kept them out all the time, the book tucked under one arm or into the front of his breeches. His right ear soon became spattered with ink due to his habit of placing the quill there when not actually writing. It gave him a jaunty air, poking out from behind his ear like the feather of a new cap.

There was the day we crossed a great meadow without seeing any trees at all. Ironheart made notations about butterflies and picked wildflowers to press between the pages of his book. And, though the day was bright and clear, it was also the one in which I felt a shadow slowly begin to take shape in the back of my mind. In the depths of my heart.

This isn't the way it's supposed to be, I thought. Though *How can this be the way it's supposed to be?* is probably more precise. I had come to la Forêt expecting it to be dark and dangerous and terrible. Or at the very least to hold the possibility for those things inside it, as I held such things inside me. So far, with the exception of that first hailstorm, I'd seen nothing of them.

The longer I walked, the more certain I became. The current situation couldn't last for very much longer, because it just couldn't be right.

And as for Ironheart, he'd forgotten all about his beautiful sleeping princess, as far as I could tell. He hadn't mentioned her in days, seemingly content to simply ramble through the Forest making notes. Surely true love was a thing not so easily distracted. Though how he could actually *be* in love with a girl he'd never even met was a thing I still hadn't managed to figure out.

All in all, I was becoming what my nurse would have called *out of sorts*. So I suppose it was only reasonable that out-of-the-way things began to happen, for that is how the world works, or so I've always been told. Thinking about dark and troublesome things, wondering when they'll come to pay you a visit, turns out to be the very best way to call them to your side.

It all started when I picked the fight.

A thing I'm hardly proud to admit, but as I've promised to tell the truth, there's really no way to leave it out.

It happened on a day that started out much like any other, but turned out to be the one on which I decided that I'd simply had enough. The day of the never-ending apple orchard.

We came across it early in the morning of what I was pretty sure was our fifth day in the Forest. A number that felt significant, somehow. Hadn't it taken six steps to cross the boundary between la Forêt and the world I knew? Therefore, might it not make sense that it would take six days to reach its heart, as well? In which case, tomorrow could be eventful in ways that were impossible to predict.

Not that anything about la Forêt had been all that predictable so far.

The first trees we passed were all in bud. Aside from noting that they were different from the trees of the day before, I don't think even Ironheart thought all that much about them. The land through which we walked had grown hilly overnight—soft green rolls of earth with tiny valleys nestled like jewels in between them. A land like the gentle swells of the ocean, swells just high enough to hide what was beyond them. We couldn't see what was up ahead until we'd reached the top of each rise.

Shortly before noon, a strange sound began to fill our ears, a deep low buzzing. Ironheart lifted his head like a dog on a scent.

"What's that?" he inquired.

"How should I know?" I said, my tone already grumpy. I was getting tired of all this upping and downing. To me, it felt as if la Forêt was playing tricks again, when it knew quite well I wanted things to be clear and straightforward. "I can't see any farther ahead than you can, you know."

Ironheart glanced at me, a furrow between his brows. But I could tell that only about half of the frown was for me. The rest of his attention was already fixed on whatever lay beyond the next rise.

"Come on, let's go find out," he said.

"Wait a minute," I cautioned. "You don't—"

But by then, of course, he was off and running. I watched him top the rise in front of us, then stop dead, his hands hanging loosely at his sides. On a spurt of adrenaline, I followed him up, my hand reaching for the knife at my boot.

It was more apple orchard. But such an orchard as

could exist only within the boundaries of la Forêt. Which, of course, is really just another way of saying, an apple orchard the likes of which I'd never seen before.

Below us, the land flattened out into the broadest valley we had seen that day. It was round, like an enormous bowl. The trees closest to us were all in bloom, their scent rising up to meet us, a great fragrant cloud so strong it was almost visible, and brushed with just the faintest hint of rose.

"They're bees," said Ironheart. For naturally it was they who were making the buzzing. I'd never seen so many before, not even among my father's orchards. So many they almost covered the blossoms.

But even this was not the most remarkable thing. More amazing still were the trees that stood in the very center of the bowl, for these were not in blossom. Even from a distance, we could see ripe fruit hanging from their boughs. They had been planted in a great pattern of diamonds, each comprised of trees bearing fruit of one color. Green. Red. Gold. It was like looking down on a tapestry made entirely of apple trees.

Beyond even these, at the bowl's far edge, were trees whose limbs were stark and bare, as if in the midst of winter. An entire season of growing in microcosm.

"I don't understand this place," I said.

Ironheart nodded, his expression sober. "Neither do I." Then the smile that never seemed to be far from his face burst out across it. "But I do know I want to find out if those apples taste as good as they look. Come on."

And so I followed him down.

The air among the blooming trees was so thick it made me dizzy. The apples themselves, when we finally reached them, were so plump and ripe the juice all but burst from their skins as they hung upon the trees. Ironheart picked two of each kind and stowed them carefully in his knapsack. (Away from the pinecones, I assumed.) Then he plucked a golden one and held it up against my cheek.

"Look, Aurore. It matches your hair."

"Don't be silly," I said, but I took it from him anyway. I polished it absently against my shirt while I watched him dash into the trees the next diamond over, scouting until he'd found the biggest, reddest apple of them all. He devoured it in six enormous bites, the juice running down his chin. A look of wonder filled his face.

"It's like the water," he said. "More of what it is. I wonder how each color tastes different from the next."

"Try it and see," I said, and tossed the golden apple to him. As it arced through the air, it flashed in the sun, bright as a coin. This one he devoured in only four bites, as it was smaller than the one before.

"It tastes like honey warmed in the sun." And the green tasted of spring, or so he said. But, although Ironheart urged me to, I couldn't bring myself to eat

a single bite. It was as if I feared that, if I did, I'd fall
under some spell. Voluntarily put my hand in a trap.
The beauty of the apple orchard had only increased
my fears. You draw more flies with honey, or so I've
always been told.

I did consent to let Ironheart stuff several more
apples into my knapsack. In case I changed my mind
later, he said. When I pointed out he had some of his
own, he loftily explained that the ones in his pack
were for scientific purposes, not for eating.

It was late in the day when we reached the outskirts of the orchard, the limbs of the barren trees on
the rim looking like stiff, aching arms that stretched
toward the darkening sky. By mutual consent, we
halted. Beyond the orchard lay a great bank of mist.
We could not see our way forward.

"I think we should stop here for the night,"
Ironheart said. "Find a place to make camp in the
orchard. There's no sense blundering around in the
dark."

"All right," I said. *Tomorrow, the sixth day will dawn,*
I thought. A day I was pretty sure would prove to be
significant, one way or another.

"Let's go back a little ways," Ironheart suggested
suddenly. "I don't like the idea of camping on the edge
of anything." He eyed the fogbank suspiciously. "It
feels—I'm not quite sure—too exposed."

At this, I felt the tension that had been riding me
all day ease a bit. *It isn't just me. He feels it too,* I
thought.

"All right," I said again, as we began to make our way back toward the center of the orchard. It was well and truly dark now, a night with no moon, no stars. We stumbled along for a few more rows of trees. Then I heard Ironheart cry out, and then a *thud* as he hit the ground.

I had the knife out of my boot in the time it took to blink. "What is it?" I cried.

For a moment, I thought I heard him swearing under his breath. "Just my own big feet," he said after a moment. "Or big foot, I should say. And a gopher hole." In the dim light, I could see him stand up, and dust himself off. "I'm going to take it for a sign. This is far enough."

I slid the knife back into its sheath. "Over here," I said, walking closer to the nearest row of trees. "It's not so bumpy." Together, we shucked off our knapsacks and settled to the ground, wrapping ourselves in our cloaks. "Ironheart, I've been wondering something."

"Well, it's about time," he said. "A little longer and the suspense might have killed me. You've been brooding all day, Aurore."

"I have not either," I said, feeling a spurt of irritation. "Just because I don't treat every single day like it's a lark."

"You know perfectly well I don't do that," he said in a reasonable tone. A thing which caused a second spurt of irritation to shoot through my veins. There's nothing worse than being spoken to patiently when you're well and truly cross. It's enough to make even a grown person feel like a child.

"Stop trying to pick a fight, Aurore," Ironheart went on. "Tell me what it is you wonder instead."

"All right," I said. "Since you asked me: How will you know when we've reached the heart of the Forest? Do you even know what it looks like?"

"Not really," he admitted, and though his features were just a blur, I could imagine him making a self-deprecating face in the darkness. "I guess I just assumed it would be obvious. That there would be a castle or a bower or something. I don't think a beautiful princess would just be sleeping out in the open, do you?"

"What if there isn't a beautiful sleeping princess?" I asked. "What if she's not so beautiful, or she's wide awake, or somebody else got there first and she's gone?"

"No," he said at once. "She's going to be there, and I'm going to bring her the kiss of true love."

"But you can't *know* that," I protested. If I'd been standing up, it's likely I'd have stomped my foot. "You can't possibly know for sure."

"Yes, I can, Aurore."

"How?" I challenged.

"Because it's what I feel in my heart," Ironheart said, his tone telling me he thought this should be obvious. "My heart knows she's going to be there, even if my mind can't explain how."

"But can't you see how preposterous that is?" I

said, suddenly appalled to realize I was fighting back an impulse to cry. How could he be so certain love would be waiting, when I wasn't certain of anything at all? "How can you love someone you've never even met? It can't even be love at first sight!"

"I don't have to meet her," he answered. "I've known her my whole life."

"Ironheart, you're talking about a story," I said, striving to make my own tone reasonable now. "A romantic fairy tale told to you by your grandfather. For all you know, he made it up to give you a purpose. Make you feel good about yourself. It's not the same as loving a real live human being."

"She's real to me," said Ironheart, his voice sharp. "And my grandfather never mentioned any fairies."

"All right," I said. "What does she look like?"

"What difference does that make?" exclaimed Ironheart. "What she looks like isn't important. I care about what's in her heart."

"But you can't *know* what's in her heart! That's my whole point!"

"I can, too," said Ironheart. "It's the match for what's in mine. Just because you don't feel that way about anybody doesn't mean I can't."

"It does so, because nobody can. And that's a terrible thing to say. You don't know anything about my feelings."

"I can so, and you asked for it," shot back Ironheart. "What's gotten into you today, Aurore? I'd have said the quest was going fine, until today."

"It's *not* a quest," I all but yelled, as I jumped to my feet. "It's a walk in the park. A quest is supposed to test your mettle, make you prove yourself. How many obstacles have we faced so far? How many challenges?"

"Counting you right this minute, you mean?"

"Ha ha. Very funny. Okay, answer me this: How many steps did it take you to get into the Forest?"

Even in the dark, I could see him drop his head into his hands. "What kind of a question is that? You think I was counting?"

I took a deep breath, striving for calm. "When I got close to the Forest," I said, "there was a ring around it, of dry grass. Sort like a moat without the water. As if it marked the place where the regular world ended and the Forest began. It seemed to me that it went all the way around it."

Ironheart lifted his head. "All right, yes," he said. "You're right. I remember. What about it?"

"How many steps did it take you to cross it?"

"What difference does that make?"

"Look, if you can't remember, just say so."

"All right, all right, let me think a minute." He took almost exactly sixty seconds to come up with his answer. I know because I counted. "Half a dozen. I remember because I thought it would take less. It didn't look that far, and my legs are kind of long."

"Six steps," I said. "That's the same number it took me. How many days have we been walking through the Forest?"

"Five," Ironheart answered promptly. "I know that because I've been taking notes, by the way. Which only goes to show they haven't been a waste of time."

There was another moment of silence. "Oh," he said. And then again, "Oh. So you think . . ."

"That tomorrow will be the day we reach the heart of the Forest."

"What's so bad about that?" he asked at once. "Isn't that what we've been trying to do all along? And how do you know it will be six days? Why not some multiple of six? Twelve? Eighteen? Twenty-four?"

"It's going to be six," I said.

"Oh, I see," he replied. "You mean you just *know*. In your heart."

"Something like that," I said.

"So you can do it but I can't, is that it?"

"Now who's trying to pick a fight?"

"I'm not picking a fight," Ironheart said, his tone so reasonable it made me want to kick something. "I'm defending myself. Just because I'm pointing out the flaws in your logic is no reason to start accusing me of things. There's no shame in being afraid, you know, Aurore. If you are, you should just say so."

"I am *not* afraid," I said. Though, of course that was the moment I realized how desperately I was. Afraid of what awaited me in the heart of the Forest. Afraid that it would be something shining, quick, and sharp. That had just one reason for its existence: to draw from me one bright drop of blood.

Whatever waited for me in the heart of la Forêt,

I was sure it wasn't love. And suddenly, the thought that tomorrow Ironheart might embrace his happiness, while the only thing I embraced was fear was more than I could bear.

"I'm finished with this conversation," I said. "I'm not talking to you anymore."

"Oh, for heaven's sake, Aurore!" Ironheart exclaimed. "Will you listen to yourself?"

I stomped to a tree a little ways away from the one under which he was sitting, desperately praying I didn't step right into another gopher hole. It's hard to be on your high horse when you're falling on your face. There, I sat down in a huff and put my back against the tree.

"Fine," Ironheart said. "If that's the way you want it. But don't blame me if you catch cold."

"I don't know why you bother to keep speaking," I said. "Nobody's paying attention to a word you say."

I heard him sigh. "Oh, go to sleep, Aurore. If you're not in a better mood tomorrow, I'm going on without you."

As I sat with my back against the rough bark of the apple tree, I wondered suddenly if that hadn't been exactly what I wanted all along.

That night, I dreamed of home.

At first I thought it was the nightmare, come to haunt me even within the confines of la Forêt. But, even from inside the dream, I knew that this was wrong. It was true the dreams began in much the same way, though instead of actually being in the palace, I was in the village below, moving toward it. The sense that I was searching for something I had lost was as strong as ever. But, in this dream, I knew I was myself. I was Aurore.

Instead it was the land around me which seemed to have changed, though at first the alterations were so subtle I hardly noticed. But gradually it came to me that, everywhere I looked, the colors seemed brighter than I remembered. The crops and livestock, taller and fatter. The whitewash on the village cottages just a little more white. Prosperity and contentment had cast their mantles out across the land, gleaming satin cloaks of green and gold. Peace and happiness seemed to reign in every direction.

The stewards have done well, I thought.

And with this thought, I reached the palace and stopped. For I saw that the walls that had once kept it locked away from the world outside had been torn down, a thing I knew had long been a dream of Papa's. An elaborate wrought-iron gate marked the entrance to the palace grounds, but it stood wide open. A white rose and a red rose clambered up either side as if racing to embrace one another. Their scent circled around my head as I passed beneath them, heading for the kitchen garden.

It looked much as I remembered, save that it was more abundant, just as everything was. The paths between the rows of plants were broader, covered in nutshells that made cheerful cracking noises as I walked along. And beside each plant was a marker, telling what its name was. As if someone had anticipated the curiosity of all the little girls who had come after me, of royal birth or not.

Beside a plant with leaves mottled green and purple, I knelt down. I had no need to read the marker to know what it was. Not only did I remember for myself, but it seemed to me that I could hear my cousin's voice, clear as the peal of a church bell in the back of my mind.

"That is sage, Aurore."

Sage, which even as a child I had known meant *wise. You and your descendants have done well, Oswald*, I thought.

For surely the prosperity I saw all around me was my cousin's handiwork, proof positive that he had taken our final conversation straight into his heart. No other combination of things could have produced the peace and bounty I saw around me, for those things required both wisdom and love. And patience, also.

This was the world my departure had created. A future both shining and glorious. This was the gift I had given my people by holding my love for them safe and strong within my heart.

Yet even as this thought came to me, I began to weep, for suddenly I perceived that this bright and shining future held no place in it for me. There was no one left whom I had known and loved. And as my tears fell unchecked into the fertile earth, it seemed to me that, at long last, I understood the unhappiness that had always seemed to dwell inside my cousin Oswald.

Had he not been surrounded by all that he desired, yet been undesired in return? Rising each day to live in a world in which he knew he had no place. And so, just as she had spoken her spell first, so it seemed to me that Cousin Jane would have the last word now. For though Chantal's spell might save my life, it would doom me to live in a world which owed its very existence to the fact that I hadn't been in it. Like Oswald, I would be surrounded by others, yet always alone.

"Aurore," I heard a voice say. "*You're dreaming. Wake up.*"

There were hands upon my shoulders, shaking me. Then I felt myself pulled into a pair of arms. "*Don't weep, Aurore. I'm here,*" the voice said.

And at that, I woke up, and knew where I was. I was in la Forêt, at the base of an apple tree, held tightly in Ironheart's arms.

"I wasn't weeping," I said. "I never cry."

"Well, at least I know you're awake now," said Ironheart.

I tried to sit up, but he pushed my head back down against his chest. "Stop fussing," he said. "I've had enough conflict for one day. Just lie still, Aurore. Try relying on me for once. Think of it this way: I owe you for building five nights worth of fires."

Part of me was tempted to argue. I hated to seem

weak, but he did have a point. Besides, the dream had left me shaking and Ironheart felt solid and warm.

"I'm sorry I was so disagreeable," I mumbled against his chest.

"I'm sorry you were too," said Ironheart. At this I tried to lift my head again, but he held it firmly in place with the back of one hand. "Shut up and go to sleep, Aurore. We can argue again in the morning, if you still want to."

And so I gave up and went to sleep in the shelter of his arms, my head pressed against the rhythm of his heart. All through the night, it seemed to me that it pounded out his name. One I was beginning to believe was his true one after all.

Ironheart. Ironheart. Ironheart.

⚜Fifteen⚜

When I awoke the next morning, I was alone. My head was resting on a great tree root instead of where I thought it would be, which was Ironheart's shoulder. I had a crick in my neck I was sure would remain for the rest of the day, a thing I certainly intended to mention in no uncertain terms.

Just as soon as I found him.

I stood up and stretched, then shouldered my knapsack and wrapped both cloaks around me. He'd left me his, which I had to admit was very considerate. The air was sharp, though the sky was clear even in the early morning. It was the kind of day Nurse always said reminded her of the one on which I had been born. A day like a beautiful wild animal with a glossy coat and a mouth full of teeth. The kind of day where anything could happen, so you'd better watch out.

The sixth day since I'd come to the Forest.

I found Ironheart standing at the very edge of the apple orchard, staring straight ahead and frowning.

"Oh, good, you're awake. Come and tell me what you make of this," he said as I moved to stand beside him.

I studied it.

"Whatever it is, it's green," I said. "And yes, thank you, I did sleep well. Except for the crick in my neck that I'm sure is all your fault. Good morning."

At this, he gave me his full attention, turning to me with a smile and slinging one arm around my shoulders. "Good morning, Aurore. I can see that it's green. But what else is it? That's what I really want to know."

We stared ahead in silence for a moment. "Well," I said. "It's obviously a hedge of some sort."

It was taller than either of us and extended in both directions as far as my eyes could see. Even from where we stood, some distance away, I could see that its branches were filled with both buds and thorns. As we watched, the sun struck the section closest to us, causing it to suddenly burst into bloom. Blossom after blossom of a pink as pale as the first flush of light in the sky.

"Roses," Ironheart exclaimed suddenly. "It's a hedge made of roses." I could tell by the sound of his voice that he was relieved. More than that, he was delighted. Roses and sleeping princesses were the sorts of things that almost always went together.

"It's in our way," I said, my own voice grumpy.

He chuckled. "How can it be in our way when we don't really know where we're going? Besides, I should think you'd be happy about something like this. You were the one who wanted a challenge."

I didn't have a particularly good answer for that remark, as he happened to be right, so I decided to ignore it. Instead, I took off his cloak and handed it to him.

"All right," I said. "Let's see if we can go around it."

After some debate about which direction to go, we went to the right and walked for several hours, the sun inching ever higher in the sky and the rose hedge blooming as we moved along it. There were white roses, then lavender, and then a gold that Ironheart said exactly matched the color of my hair. And finally a vivid red that reminded me of the fate that awaited me. The prick of a finger, followed by one bright drop of blood. As we walked along, we munched apples and the last of Ironheart's cheese, until the sight of the red roses made me lose my appetite.

"Do you suppose this was here last night?" Ironheart mused as we halted about midday. With the sun directly overhead, the rose hedge was a riot of color. "And we just couldn't see it because of the mist?"

I nodded. "It's too tall to have just sprung up overnight." I watched a branch move as if stretching in the sun, an action I swear made it taller. "Though, considering where we are, I suppose anything is possible."

Ironheart cocked his head. "I don't think it's just a boundary," he said. "I think there's something inside it."

"You mean your princess," I said.

He shrugged as if what I'd said wasn't important, but I saw that his face had colored. "Why not? You just said it yourself: Considering where we are, anything is possible."

"Well, if there is something inside, there has to be a way in," I said. "I don't think we can just climb over it."

"I've been thinking the same thing," Ironheart nodded. He fell silent, studying the hedge. "I wonder when we'll find it."

"Probably when the Forest wants us to," I said. Or when we wanted it enough. "Come on. Let's keep going."

We found it about an hour later, though the opening was so small we almost walked right by it.

"Ouch," I heard Ironheart suddenly exclaim. He stopped walking abruptly. A long branch of roses whose blossoms were the same color orange as the sun when it set had become entangled in the hood of his cloak. "Help me, will you please, Aurore?"

I eyed the branch, specifically, its thorns. They were small, but I knew better than to assume that meant they weren't sharp. I took off my pack, fished out my leather gloves and pulled them on. A moment later, Ironheart was free, the branch bobbing above his head as if laughing at some secret joke.

"Thank you," Ironheart said, as he turned around. "I can't think why—" He stopped speaking as abruptly as he'd stopped walking, his eyes growing wide. I think I knew what it was before I even turned to follow his gaze.

Just below the branch that had snared his cloak there was a break in the hedge, so subtle that if I hadn't been staring straight at it, I would never have noticed. The hedge still continued as straight as ever, but one section was offset, as if it had taken a step backward. If you were careful and turned sideways, you'd be able to slip in between the two sections of hedge.

"What do you think?" asked Ironheart.

"I think it's what we've been waiting for," I said. Whether I was ready for it or not.

"I'll go first," said Ironheart.

He pulled his hood up over his head, gathered his cloak in close to his body, then stepped to the hedge, turned, and scooted sideways. A moment later, I heard his sharp intake of breath.

"Are you all right?" I called.

"I think you'd better come and see this," he said.

I followed his example. A moment later, I was standing by his side. In front of us was another series of hedges, moving off in different directions. Branching every which way like a series of corridors.

"It's a maze," I said.

"I knew it," Ironheart whispered, his eyes shining. "I knew there was more to that hedge than met the eye. We're almost there, Aurore. Can you feel it?"

Oh yes, I thought. I could feel my skin prickle, the way it did when danger approached. For, no matter how long it took to solve them, all mazes had one thing in common: They had a heart. And, in that moment, it seemed plain to me that the heart of the maze and the heart of the Forest were one and the same.

Now all we had to do was to find it.

❖Sixteen❖

$\mathcal{A}$s it turned out, it didn't take nearly as long as I thought it might, which is the way things sometimes go. The anticipation takes longer than the actual event. In this case, it was as if even the Forest was in a hurry to get things over with, now that we'd gotten so close. Perhaps it feared that we would change our minds at the last moment. Decide to turn around and go back home instead of heading forward toward the goal.

Ironheart went first, insisting we go to the right as we had first thing that morning, his voice happy and excited when I asked him why. This wasn't a mysterious puzzle, like la Forêt itself. This was a puzzle he knew how to solve.

"Because that's the way a maze works," he said, as we reached the first intersection. Without hesitation, he moved to the right once more. "Or at least, some of them. The ones constructed the way this one is. I can tell just by looking at it. The royal gardener and I once made a series of studies."

We came to a second intersection and he turned right yet again, walking so close to the hedge he almost brushed it with his shoulder in spite of the ever present thorns. After that, the maze became more complex and he picked up the pace, weaving through a series of twists and turns so swiftly I practically had to jog to keep up.

"For heaven's sake," I said. "Whatever's waiting for us isn't going anywhere. Slow down."

"The hedge on our right is continuous," he called back over his shoulder, continuing his explanation of how he knew how to get where we were going. "There are no breaks in it anywhere. All we have to do is follow it, always keeping it *on* our right, and it will lead us to the maze's heart. It's really incredibly simple, once you know the trick."

I suppose I don't have to tell you that this was the moment that disaster struck. Never say a thing is simple, even if you know it is. Because as soon as you do, things get complicated. You might as well just come right out and invite something you'd rather not meet to rear its ugly head and bite you. Or in this case, scratch you, which is what happened next. As Ironheart turned back around, he turned a corner at the same time and one long cane of thorns, hidden by the turn in the maze, slashed across his face.

He gave a cry that had my heart leaping straight up into my throat. I sprinted toward him, already shucking off my knapsack.

"How bad is it? Let me see!" I said.

He had one hand—his left hand—pressed against the same side of his face. As if, even in wounding him, the maze had deliberately left his right side unimpaired. I could see bright drops of blood leaking out through his fingers—the same color as the blossoms covering the bushes all around us, as the thorns on the cane that even now arched above us, still quivering with the force of their contact.

"It's all right. I'm all right," he gasped.

"You're not all right," I insisted, dragging on his hand. "Ironheart, I can't help you if you won't let me see."

To my amazement, he jerked back. "Not yet," he snapped. "Not until we reach the heart."

"That's crazy," I said. "You're hurt. You have to let me help you *now*." But I was talking to his back.

"When we reach the heart," he said again as he staggered off. "Not before that."

And so we completed our journey to the heart of the maze, the heart of the Forest, with Ironheart weaving like a drunkard and me trailing along behind him, following the bright drops of blood that slipped from his fingers and fell to the grass like so many scarlet bread crumbs. To this day, I can't tell you how long it took, though he was right about the way the maze worked, of course. After what seemed like endless twisting and turning, we rounded one final corner and there it was. I'm not sure quite what I'd expected. Something stately and royal, I suppose. Or at the very least something that reeked of storybook magic. A smooth square of perfectly green grass with a pavilion made of crystal in its very center and a fountain splashing water as clear as diamonds. Or perhaps a woodland glen inhabited by both a lion and a unicorn.

La Forêt being what it was, the thing it held within its heart was neither of those things. It was simply a garden, and a practical one at that, with herbs and vegetables planted in tidy rows. The only structure I could see was an old wooden potting shed. The closest thing to a fountain was a brick-lined well. And the only place where a princess might have slept for a hundred minutes, let alone a hundred years, was a bench with a flowered cushion for her head at one end. On the other end lay a straw hat with a bright blue ribbon tied around the crown, as if whoever tended this place had just taken it off and gone for a morning stroll.

But of the gardener herself, there was no sign.

"No," I heard Ironheart choke out. His steps faltered, and he came to a halt. "*No.*"

My heart was knocking against my ribs so hard I thought it might break. With his sorrow, not with my own.

"Sit down," I said, putting my hands on his shoulders and pushing him downwards. "Let me see your face."

His legs folded like a house of twigs, his hands flopping useless in his lap. "She's not here. She's not here, Aurore."

"Don't be ridiculous, of course she's here," I said, making my voice as brisk as I could. "You don't think a princess is going to sleep for a hundred years outside.

She'd catch her death of cold long before her handsome prince could even set out, let alone arrive."

Not so bad. It's not so bad, I thought. Though it had bled fiercely during our sprint, most of the bleeding had stopped by now, and the wound had somehow missed his eye. It started midforehead, then slanted downward across the left side of his face. I was pretty sure the thing that had saved his eye had been the bridge of his nose. But the cut was deep, especially across his cheek, and would need to be cleansed and stitched.

"Sit there," I said. "I'll get some water from the well."

"No," he protested, trying to get to his feet. "I can't just sit here. I have to find her, Aurore."

"And so you will," I said. "But you can't do it looking like you've just been attacked by brigands. You want to bring her the kiss of true love, not scare her half to death. Wouldn't you say she's already been through enough?"

"You're right. Of course you're right," he said. "It's just—"

"Sit still," I commanded, making my voice as stern as I could. "The sooner you let me do this, the sooner you can get on with your quest."

But as I started to rise, he caught my hand. "She is here, isn't she? I will find her, won't I, Aurore?"

"Of course you will," I said, though I felt the pain of doubt close like a vise around my heart. "Isn't it the thing for which you were born?"

"That's right. It is," he said. And then he smiled, a thing that caused a sluggish line of blood to ooze from his cut at its deepest point.

"I'll be right back," I said. I made for the well. After returning with most of a bucket of water, I knelt down beside him, then rummaged in my knapsack for my extra shirt and the healing supplies I had brought along.

"This will probably hurt," I said, as I used my knife to hack one of the sleeves off the shirt. "I'm sorry, but I don't think it can be helped."

Ironheart attempted a smile. "It's all right," he said. "Really, I'm tougher than I look."

I paused in the act of dunking the sleeve in the water and met his eyes. "No, you're not."

He opened his mouth to protest, then closed it again as he realized what I'd meant. "Thank you," he said. "I think that's about the nicest thing anybody's ever said to me, Aurore."

"Just don't let it go to your head," I remarked. "There's nothing worse than a man who thinks too well of himself."

Then swiftly I laid the damp cloth against his face while he was still chuckling. He jerked once, his eyes telling me he knew exactly what I'd done, then calmed. Carefully I washed the dried blood from his face, working slowly and patiently until I felt sure the wound was as clean as I could make it.

"I'm going to have to stitch your cheek," I said.

Somehow, he managed to make a face. "A thing

you've no doubt done a million times before."

"A million and one," I said, as I deftly threaded my needle, grateful for the first time for Maman's insistence that I learn to use one properly.

He chuckled and reached one hand out to grasp mine at the wrist, holding it still. "I like you, Aurore. I just wanted to say that—before whatever else is going to happen happens."

"I like you, too," I replied.

"All right," he said. "Let's get this over with."

Though the first instance of needle going through flesh gave us both a bad moment, in a matter of minutes I was snipping off the thread and the deed was done. I wove the needle through the thigh of my right pant leg, desperate to get it out of my hands before they could begin to shake, then turned to dip a fresh piece of torn shirtsleeve into the bucket.

"Here, take this," I said, leaning forward to hand it over. "The water is cold. It will help keep the swelling down. Why don't you rest for just a moment before you—"

I felt a small, bright spear of pain, for all the world like the sting of a bee, shoot through my right hand as I sat back upon my heels and my hand brushed against my thigh. Turning it over, I could see something exactly in the center of the pad of my right forefinger.

One bright drop of blood.

My eyes dropped to where I'd tucked the needle into the top of my pants. *You great idiot, Aurore.* And so the fate I'd been waiting my whole life for was upon me, and of course I'd brought it on myself.

"Ouch," I said softly. And then, "I wonder what happens now?"

Ironheart took the cloth down from his face. "What is it? What's the matter, Aurore?"

There was urgency in his voice, I could hear it, but I could no longer seem to summon any sense of urgency myself. There was a strange sound filling my ears, a sound that somehow managed to sound like weeping beyond all hope of consolation and joyous shouting at the same time.

"There's something I need to tell you," I said.

"What is it?" he said, and I think I felt his hands upon my shoulders. "For the love of God, Aurore."

No longer able to answer, I looked up into his face, and, as I did so, for the very first time, I saw what and who it was I carried, strong and safe, inside my heart.

Oh for heaven's sake, I thought. *How on earth could I have missed a thing like that? I wished that I had said something, but I suppose it's too late now.*

Then my eyes went blind and my mind went blank. And in my ears, a sound like church bells ringing on a cold, clear dawn.

❧Seventeen❧

𝐼 awoke to a thing I'd never felt before. Something was moving across my face, fierce and demanding. And a voice was saying my name in exactly the same way. "Aurore. Aurore." Then I felt something touch my lips. Once. Twice. Then a third time, each with growing desperation, and realized what I felt were lips themselves. I was being kissed.

"For the love of God, don't leave me," the voice said. "Come back, Aurore."

"All right," I said, struggling to open my eyes. They didn't seem to want to obey my mind's instructions, as if they knew better than I that being closed was their proper position. A position they'd been in for a very long time.

"I can hear you. My ears still work. There's no need to shout."

Whoever held me made a strange sound and pressed me against his chest, rocking me back and forth the way you do a small child.

"I'm going to knock you senseless as soon as you're completely awake," he said.

At this I struggled to sit up, for it seemed to me it was a voice I knew. And no sooner had this thought occurred than I opened my eyes. The sun was so dazzling that I immediately shut them again.

"Ironheart?"

"Well, who else would it be?" he asked, his tone more than a little aggrieved. "What on earth happened? You scared me to death, Aurore."

"You kissed me," I said, opening my eyes once more. They watered like anything, but this time I managed to keep them open. "Did you kiss me?"

"All right. Okay. Yes, I did," said Ironheart, and even through my watery eyes I could see the way his face colored.

"There's no need to get all bothered about it. The truth is, I sort of lost my head. One minute you were fine. The next you were saying all these things that didn't make any sense at all. Then you keeled right over. I've never seen anybody go as white and still as you did. I thought—that is—I was afraid that you were dead, or something."

"Not dead. Just sleeping. I was supposed to sleep for a hundred years," I said. And watched his mouth drop open.

"Well, it certainly *felt* like a hundred years," he said forcefully. "But that would mean—" He broke off, his eyes growing wide. "That would mean that you— that I . . . oh." He dropped his head down into his hands. "I don't understand any of this, Aurore."

"Neither do I," I said with a smile. "I do know one thing, though."

"What's that?"

"I want to go home."

"Sounds good to me," he said. "Do you suppose the Forest will let us go?"

"Your grandfather must have thought so," I said. "Otherwise, he never would have sent you on this quest."

"Good point," said Ironheart. And with that he stood up, pulling me with him. Supporting me when I swayed, as if my legs had forgotten their proper function. "Oh, my."

"What?" I asked. In answer, he simply turned me around, so that I faced back the way we'd come.

The maze was gone.

In its place were low-growing rose shrubs and wild clematis, scrambling over and through one another in great curving mounds. It was as if the maze had become an old woman, still beautiful, but bent, softened with time. Beyond the roses, the trees of la Forêt opened up to rolling pastureland. I could see the towers of a castle in the distance, their banners blowing bright against the sky.

"That's my father's castle," I said. And heard Ironheart make a sound.

"I was afraid you were going to say that," he said.

I turned in his arms to gaze up at him. "Why?"

"Because it's also the place where I grew up. This is getting stranger by the minute, Aurore."

"The sooner we get back, the better," I said.

"Right," Ironheart agreed at once. "Okay, off we go."

With that, he scooped me up into his arms and started down the hill toward the castle.

"Wait a minute!" I cried. "I'm not a sack of potatoes, in case you hadn't noticed. Put me down!"

"In a minute," he said. "And if you keep squirming like that, I'll throw you over my shoulder as if you *were* a sack of potatoes. You're still a little shaky on your feet. You just don't want to admit it. Let me help you for once, Aurore."

"You could have asked first," I grumbled, though I did stop squirming. The sentiment he'd expressed had been rather sweet.

"What for? All you would have done is to say no."

"I suppose you think you know me pretty well," I said.

"Well enough," said Ironheart with a smile.

We reached the bottom of the hill. The trees thinned out, and the pastureland began. After a few more moments of walking, we reached a road.

"Put me down, please," I said, and, at once, Ironheart obliged. As if he understood my desire to return home, if it was still home, on my own two feet. The same way I had left it behind.

"What do you suppose will happen when we get there?" I asked.

Ironheart reached down to take my hand. "I don't know. Would you rather go the other way? I suppose we could."

"No," I said swiftly, though I had to admit the offer was tempting. To put it from my mind I said, "No," once more. "I guess I just thought going home would be less mysterious than leaving it. Instead, it's more."

"I know exactly what you mean," Ironheart said, in such heartfelt agreement that I laughed in spite of myself, and suddenly, things didn't seem so bad anymore.

"I guess it's like taking medicine," I said. "The sooner you do it, the sooner you can get on to whatever comes next."

"Could be," Ironheart said. "Though I do hope it won't involve any throwing up."

"That's disgusting," I said. "Race you."

And with that, we were off.

❧Eighteen❧

It took less time than I remembered to get home from la Forêt.

Home.

Could I really still call it that? I wondered. When I was far from certain what was waiting for me there? A home is more than just a building, after all, even if that building is a castle.

Stop thinking and just keep walking. You won't know if it's home until you get there, Aurore.

The closer we got, the more settled the land around us became. What had once been open countryside was now dotted with prosperous farms. People stopped working in the fields as we passed by them, running to crowd around Ironheart. It was plain that his great quest was quite well known, a thing that soon caused people to crowd around me as well. By the time we reached the place where the castle gates stood open to all who wished to enter, we'd collected quite a throng. As we passed through them, farmers and townspeople streaming like a great living train behind us, a young man came out from the palace to meet us.

"You're back," he said to Ironheart. "You brought a girl with you." In both statements, the astonishmnent was plain in his voice.

"A princess," I said with a silent apology to both Maman and Ironheart. I knew it wasn't proper etiquette for me to speak first, but the truth was that the young man's tone irked me. He sounded so surprised. "And you must be Ironheart's brother, Valiant," I said, and watched surprise become bewilderment.

"That's right," he said. "How did you know?"

"From Ironheart's very accurate description," I said, not daring to look in Ironheart's direction, particularly when I heard him give a strangled snort.

"Grandfather wants to see you," Valiant blurted out. "He's in the audience chamber. The big one."

"Then we should go see him right away, don't you think?" I asked, giving him my very best smile. Still looking slightly bewildered, he stepped back. Ironheart and I mounted the palace steps and stepped across the threshold into the great hall, side by side.

"I think he means the royal audience chamber," Ironheart whispered as we bore left and climbed another set of stairs. "Though I can't think why Grand-père would be there. He never uses it, since he's not really a king."

"What do you mean he's not really a king?" I asked.

But any reply he might have made was cut off by a sudden fanfare of trumpets so loud and jubilant I almost clapped my hands across my ears. In the next moment, the doors to the royal audience chamber were thrown wide open, leaving Ironheart and me no choice but to go right in.

This is the very room in which I was christened, I thought. So I suppose it only made sense that this was where my journey to and from la Forêt should end. Down the length of the room Ironheart and I walked side by side, while the townspeople and farmers crowded in behind us, jostling the courtiers who were already assembled, for all the world as if they'd known we were coming.

I could hear the rustle of silks as bows and curtsies were performed all around us. I never once turned my head. All my attention was focused on the man who sat at the far end of the room, at the base of the royal dais.

Not at their top, I instantly noticed. All that rested there were two empty thrones. My father's. My mother's. I blinked rapidly, desperate to hold back a sudden rush of tears. When my eyes were clear again, the old man and I were face-to-face, and a silence more absolute than any I had ever known had followed in my wake to fill the audience chamber.

He was the oldest man that I had ever seen. Though how old that actually was, I did not know. He sat straight and vigorous, hands resting lightly upon his knees. Hair as white as the first winter snowfall tumbled across his shoulders. The unadorned chair upon which he sat was made of dark red wood, polished until it gleamed like a ruby. Papa had given me a box made from the same kind of wood, the day I turned ten. What had he called it? Ah, yes. *Rosewood.*

And at this sudden memory, I belatedly remembered my manners and sank into a curtsy, momentarily forgetting that I was wearing breeches and a shirt no doubt stained with Ironheart's blood.

"No," he said, in a clear voice. "No, you should not bow before me, Aurore."

"You know my name," I said, and, in my amazement, looked straight into his eyes. They were gray as a storm at sea, flecked with gold like unexpected sunlight. At the sight of them, my heart rolled over, once, within my chest and then lay still.

"Oswald."

He smiled then. A flash of teeth that had remained unchanged through all the years that lay between us. And now my heart reared up and then began to gallop like a horse.

"I promised that I would wait for you, did I not, little cousin?"

❖Nineteen❖

*W*ithout warning, my knees turned to water and I sank to the floor at his feet.

For heaven's sake, Aurore, I thought. *Now is hardly the time to turn all mushy.* But by now a wild trembling had seized all my limbs. I could not have stood if my life depended on it.

"Valiant," Oswald said, his voice brisk. "Bring a chair for the princess Aurore."

This was done, and I was seated, with Ironheart standing beside me. Then my cousin reached to take my hand in his. And at this it seemed to me that he began to tremble also, though before his hands had been steady and sure.

"I'm sorry, Aurore," he said. "I should have realized that it would be a shock. It's just—"

"That you've been waiting for a hundred years," I filled in for him. I sat back, and he released my hand. I shook my head, hoping the action would convince my brain cells to function. "Even with all the magic there is around here, I still don't understand how any of this is possible."

"Many things are possible, if you desire them enough," my cousin said simply. At which my mind calmed and I remembered a thing I had forgotten.

"Ironwill," I said. "Isn't that what they call you?"

"Indeed, they do," said Oswald. "Iron seems to run in the family. Tell me, what do you make of my grandson?"

I answered without hesitation. "That although it may not have been the intention at the time, he is well-named also."

"Ah!" Oswald exclaimed. "I was hoping you would think so. You will marry him and live happily ever after, then," he said, but this time, his eyes slid away from mine. At my side, I felt Ironheart go perfectly still. And now, at last, the trembling in my body ceased and I understood my story's outcome. For what I held in my heart was as clear to me as a sudden glimpse of starlight on a cloudy night.

"I can't do that," I said softly. "If it pains either of you, I can only say that I am sorry."

Oswald's eyes jerked to mine. "But . . . ," he began.

I leaned forward just far enough to place my hands on his. "The answer is no, cousin. There are many things that I would do for you, that I *will* do," I said. "But this cannot be one of them. Though make no mistake, Ironheart is as fine a prince as any princess could wish for," I went on, raising my voice. "But to live happily ever after, there must be love, and true love at that."

"But . . . ," Oswald said again.

"Be quiet," I said firmly. "Or your iron will will have gained you nothing. I'm trying to say that it's *you* I love, Oswald."

And I leaned forward the rest of the way and pressed my lips to his before he could try to get another word in edgewise.

I felt his hands come up to grasp me by the shoulders, as they'd done the night when I left home. The sound was in my ears again, the same I'd heard when I'd pricked my finger in the Forest. But now the weeping faded away, leaving only one pure voice, singing high and joyful. Then, even that grew silent as the kiss ended and I opened my eyes. There were tears in Oswald's. And extraordinary as this was, it still wasn't the greatest cause for amazement. For my cousin was transformed.

No longer old, but young.

His outward form once more matched the image of him I had carried in my heart for so very long. For this was what I had seen in the moment before my sleep began. It was Oswald I carried in my heart. And so it was that the words my godmother Chantal had uttered on the day of my christening at last made sense. The power of her magic had snatched me from death. But it was the power of my own love which would give me the life I wanted.

All around us, I could hear a great commotion among those assembled in the room. I kept my eyes on Oswald's. And so I knew the exact moment he saw himself reflected in them.

"Sweet heavens," he whispered. "Sweet merciful, mercurial Aurore. You are, and always have been, my strongest magic."

"Not me," I said. "Us. Together."

For who could deny, literally in the face of so much wonder, that love was the greatest magic of them all?

❧ Twenty ❧

*L*ate that afternoon, I walked in the garden with Ironheart. The kitchen garden, to be exact. The same one in which I'd taken my first steps into the world, so long ago now. Oswald and I were to be married the next day, with as little pomp and as much celebration as possible. I suppose there were those who considered such haste unseemly. But then neither of us had ever cared very much what other people thought. And for ourselves, it seemed to us, in particular to Oswald, that the waiting we had already endured was more than long enough.

"Aurore," Ironheart said, as he folded his long form onto a bench beneath a row of orange trees. "Will you tell me something?"

"Of course I will," I said, as I sat down beside him. Indeed, I had a feeling I knew what was coming.

"If you hadn't known you loved Grand-père, do you think—that is—I've been wondering—"

"Of course I would have," I said.

He poked at the dirt with one booted foot. "Honestly? You aren't just saying that to sort of soften the blow?"

"You can probably answer that one yourself," I said. "Does that sound like something I might do?"

He gave a snort of laughter before he could stop himself. "All right," he said. "You've convinced me. I hope you'll be very happy, Aurore."

I linked my arm through his. "As happy as I hope you'll be someday. Come on now, admit it. You don't really love me, either. Not in a happily ever after kind of way."

"Don't I?" he said, then heaved a great sigh. "All right, it's true, I don't." There was a small but potent silence. "I thought it would make me miserable to say that," he went on after a moment. "Instead I feel much better."

"Listening to your heart and telling the truth about it does that," I said.

He made a face. "You're not going to get all know-it-all on me, are you? Because if you are, I'm going to Grand-père right now and tell him he'd be much happier marrying you off to Valiant."

"Don't tell me *both* my grandsons want to steal my bride away from me," Oswald's voice said. And there he was, suddenly standing beside us.

Ironheart jumped, then shook his head. "Did you hear him coming?"

"No," I answered. "But then sneaking up on people always was one of his best talents. Very well," I said, smiling up at Oswald. "We won't tell you. I'll just choose the one I want and run away with him. We'll write when we get to wherever it is we're going."

"I'd like to see you try," said Oswald. "You couldn't

bear to leave me again. You may as well just come right out and admit it, Aurore."

"Easy enough," I said. "Considering I never wanted to leave you in the first place."

I heard him catch his breath. And, just for a moment, he closed his eyes. When he opened them again, all I could see was gold. There was no gray in them at all.

"You have to warn me before you say things like that," he said. "You make me lose my balance, Aurore."

"That's just because you're so old," I said, as comfortingly as I could. "Here." I scooted over. "I think the bench is big enough for three. Come and sit down."

"Oh, no," said Ironheart, standing up just as Oswald slid into place beside me. "I may not be sensible like Valiant, but I know when three is one too many. Besides, I promised the royal fireworks-maker I'd help him get ready for tomorrow."

With that, he hurried off.

"I hope he doesn't blow us all sky high," Oswald said after a moment.

"It would make for a memorable occasion," I replied.

He chuckled, shifting to put one arm around me and ease my head down upon his shoulder.

"I'd say the occasion is quite memorable enough."

We sat for a moment, his fingers toying with the ends of my hair.

"Oswald," I finally said. "Will you tell me something?"

"All your life," he said.

At which I sat up straight. *"What?"*

"All your life," he repeated. "Isn't that what you wanted to know? How long I've loved you?"

"Well, yes, I suppose I did," I said. "But that wasn't what I was going to ask just now."

He gave a bark of laughter. "I tell you I've loved you since the day you were born, and you tell me you want to know something else. There's no one quite like you, is there, Aurore?"

"Well, if you don't want to tell me," I said. "If you *want* to have secrets . . ."

He laughed again. "No secrets. Not anymore. Tell me what it is you wish to know."

"Whom did you marry, since you promised it wouldn't be Marguerite de Renard? Did I know her?"

"Actually, you did," answered Oswald. "Her name was Jessica."

"Jessica," I repeated, while my mind frantically flipped through the faces of the courtiers' daughters I had known. Nothing. "Do you mean Jessica the gardener's daughter?"

"The same," said Oswald. "Our wedding day was the first time your father told me I had made him proud."

"But not the last?"

"No, not the last," answered my cousin. "On the day he rode away, he called me *son*. Aurore—about your parents."

"It's all right," I said, laying one of my hands on

top of his to silence him. "I think I know. They followed me, didn't they?"

Oswald nodded. "I don't think there's anything I could have done. They waited ten years. Long enough for your father to make certain the kingdom would be at peace—that the changes we both wished to make were going well. Actually, now that I think about it, it was surprisingly easy. The only one who really made trouble was le Renard."

"What happened?" I asked.

"He raised an army and attacked the castle, *after* your father had saved him the trouble of knocking down the walls. It didn't do a bit of good. He still lost."

"And after that?"

"There were no more problems after that. His family left the country. No one was sorry to see them go."

"And Papa and Maman?"

"It was the strangest thing," said Oswald. "One day, I looked at your father and I knew he had made up his mind. The next, he and your mother were gone. He built them a cottage just inside the borders of la Forêt. Sometimes you could see it from the outside, sometimes not. I used to ride by as often as I could, but the trees had a funny habit of moving around."

"I saw the cottage," I said. "I took shelter in it my very first night. That's where I found Ironheart. There was one of my rugs by the hearth. That really awful green one with the bumps as big as snakes."

"I remember it," said Oswald.

"It was a good place," I said. "It felt—happy—inside. Whatever the Forest holds for them, I think they are—or were—content. I will miss them, but I won't grieve for them. I don't think we were supposed to meet again. Not like you and I."

He reached to tuck a stray piece of hair back behind my ear. "Thank you for that," he said. "I love you, Aurore."

"Will you give me a gift, if I ask for it?" I said, and had the pleasure of watching his smile flash out.

"What a shameful brat you are," he said. "Very well. What?"

"I have given you my true love's kiss," I answered. "Don't you think it's time you gave me yours?"

"Past time," said my cousin.

And so he kissed me as I had him. Opening every single door inside his heart. And the kiss was like nothing I can describe. For in that moment, I both lost and gained myself.

I ceased to be Aurore and yet became her, too. For, with my heart joined with Oswald's, I became more of what I was. All the empty spaces within me filled to the brim, yet never overflowing. For true love always knows its own measure. And it is the measure of two hearts, combined.

Two hearts who need no other magic than what they hold inside them, for they have learned to beat as one.

❧Epilogue❧

(A FANCY WAY OF TYING UP
LOOSE ENDS)

The wonder of my reappearance and Oswald's transformation lasted for a year and a day, long enough for our first child to be born. Actually I suppose I should say our first children, for I bore two girls, so alike it would have been impossible to tell one from the other were it not for their eyes. One had eyes of gold flecked with silver; the other of silver flecked with gold. We named them Jane and Chantal.

Over the years, they were followed by many others, both girls and boys. All straight and fine as royal children are supposed to be. And every single one of them got to go outside as often as they desired.

Our youngest daughter is named Sage, just in case you want to know.

Not long after the birth of the twins, Valiant begged leave to depart. There were rumors of monsters ravaging distant lands. As those able to dispatch them are always in short supply, and high demand, we let him go. Not long after, he wrote from the very end of the world, to say he had dispatched a particularly horrible ogre. The people of that land were so grateful, they gave him the hand of their princess in marriage, and the kingship besides, the ogre's first despicable act having been to devour the old king, the princess's father.

Valiant's sensible, straightforward approach is much valued in the wilds at the edge of the world. He is there still, living happily ever after himself, as far as we know.

And what, you will ask, of Ironheart?

As his nature was not so straightforward as his brother's, so did the finding of his true love take a little more time. For several years, he lived with us in the palace, alternately delighting and terrifying the children with his strange and wonderful experiments, all the while filling many a leather-bound book with notes. Until the day that the king of the country just to the east sent word that he wished to build a new drawbridge and desired Ironheart's help.

While there, he rescued the king's only daughter, who turned out to be as scientifically minded as Ironheart was himself. A strange and unusual contraption she'd had specially constructed to allow her to hang suspended from trees, the better to pick their fruit, collapsed, causing her to fall and knock herself cold.

As the tree just happened to be an apple tree, and was moreover located in the heart of the maze the king had recently commissioned, and through which Ironheart just happened to be strolling, he decided perhaps he ought to give kissing the princess just one more try.

Though this failed to awaken her entirely, some water to the temples soon completed the job. When the princess's first concern was not herself but her invention, Ironheart ventured to make several suggestions concerning the design. The speed with which the princess grasped all his concepts, to say nothing of the way she elaborated upon them on the spot, soon turned their chance encounter into the world's most unusual case of love at first sight. And so he awakened a princess with true love's kiss after all.

As a wedding gift, we gave them a vast tract of land bordering her father's kingdom, so that they could live surrounded on all sides by those who love them. Her name is Marianna. Their first child was a son, and they named him Oswald.

Once a year, on the anniversary of my christening, my Oswald and I go to la Forêt. There we spend the night on which I always had bad dreams, sleeping peacefully in the cottage. To this day, we have never seen its occupants. But we bring with us mementos of our family. A rug that Jane and Chantal braided together rests before the fireplace now. It's a lovely blue, the color of a summer sky. And it lies completely flat. The year after we brought it, we arrived at the cottage to find a bowl upon the table heaped with what can only be described as a fruit still-life.

Oswald and I haven't discussed it much, but what I believe is that my parents are alive inside of la Forêt and will be for as long as I live, for they were the others I kept strong and safe inside my heart. Whether they have grown old with the years, as Oswald did, or stayed young within the boundaries of the Forest is a thing that I can never know, though I have my opinions. But I know that they are happy, because I am happy. And so I let that be enough.

People go into the Forest now, from time to time. But never more than a handful every year, and they never stay for long. Though it has ceased to be frightening, it is still mysterious, and most people find life mysterious enough without going to seek out more.

As to what happened to me there, is it possible to sleep for a hundred years in the blink of an eye? Perhaps it doesn't matter how long I actually slept, only how long I was gone. Which was certainly a hundred years, if Oswald's condition upon my return is anything to go by.

Let's see . . . what else?

Actually, nothing that I can think of. Which I think means my story has come full circle, curved around to its close. And, for once, the traditional way of ending a story is exactly the way the story of my own life turned out.

You know the words. Of course you do.

And they lived happily ever after.

Cameron Dokey is the author of more than twenty novels for young people, including the recent Simon Pulse release *The Storyteller's Daughter*. Other titles include *Hindenburg, 1937*, *Washington Avalanche, 1910*, *Buffy the Vampire Slayer: Here Be Monsters*, and *Angel: The Summoned*. Cameron's favorite reads are still those that *feel* like "Once upon a time . . ." (even if they don't actally begin that way). Her favorite place to read them is in her garden in Seattle, Washington. Another thing she loves is to hear from her readers. You can write to her at cameron.dokey@attbi.com.

Once upon a time is timely once again as fresh, quirky heroines breathe life into classic and much-loved characters.

Reknowned heroines master newfound destinies, uncovering a unique and original happily ever after. . . .

Historical romance and magic unite in modern retellings of well-loved tales.

❖❖❖❖❖

THE STORYTELLER'S DAUGHTER
by Cameron Dokey

BEAUTY SLEEP
by Cameron Dokey

SNOW
by Tracy Lynn

PUBLISHED BY SIMON PULSE

Aaron Corbet isn't a bad kid—he's just a little different.

On the eve of his eighteenth birthday, Aaron is dreaming of a darkly violent and landscape. He can hear the sounds of weapons clanging, the screams of the stricken, and another sound that he cannot quite decipher. But as he gazes upward to the sky, he suddenly understands. It is the sound of great wings beating the air unmercifully as hundreds of armored warriors descend on the battlefield.

The flapping of angels' wings.

Orphaned since birth, Aaron is suddenly discovering newfound—and sometimes supernatural—talents. But not until he is approached by two men does he learn the truth about his destiny—and his own role as a liason between angels, mortals, and Powers both good and evil—some of whom are bent on his own destruction....

the
fallen

a new series by Thomas E. Sniegoski

Book One available March 2003

From Simon Pulse

Published by Simon & Schuster

Read Cynthia Voigt's acclaimed Tillerman cycle
from beginning to end:

HOMECOMING
"An enthralling journey to a gratifying end."
—*New York Times Book Review*

DICEY'S SONG
Winner of the Newbery Medal

A SOLITARY BLUE
A Newbery Honor Book

THE RUNNER

COME A STRANGER

SONS FROM AFAR

SEVENTEEN AGAINST THE DEALER

Imagine a world where families are allowed only two children.

Illegal third children—shadow children—must live in hiding,

for if they are discovered, there is only one punishment:

Death.

Read the Shadow Children series by

MARGARET PETERSON HADDIX

Be sure to read *all* of the Alice books

The Agony of Alice

Alice in Rapture, Sort of

Reluctantly Alice

All But Alice

Alice in April

Alice In-Between

Alice the Brave

Alice in Lace

Outrageously Alice

Achingly Alice

Alice on the Outside

The Grooming of Alice

Also check out Alice on the Web at
http://www.simonsayskids.com/alice
- Read and exchange letters with
  Phyllis Reynolds Naylor!
- Get the latest news about Alice!
- Take Alice quizzes!
- Check out the Alice books
  reading group guide!

"Naylor's funny, poignant coming-of-age series . . .
has continued to serve as a kind of road map for a
girl growing up today." —*Booklist*